THE *NEW YORK TIMES* BESTSELLING AUTHOR

MAGGIE SHAYNE

"PAGE-TURNING THRILLS!"
—#1 *NY Times* Bestselling Author Karen Robards

HUNTED

SHATTERED SISTERS

suspense and laugh-out-loud one-liners from Rachel, this book will have readers engrossed until the very end." ~**RT Book Reviews** on Deadly Obsession

"This is page-turning, non-stop suspense at its finest. Shayne brings the characters to life for her readers, who will not be disappointed with this fabulously entertaining story." ~**RT Book Reviews** on Innocent Prey

"One of the strongest, most original voices in romance fiction today." ~*New York Times* bestselling author **Anne Stuart**

"Maggie Shayne is a wonderful storyteller. Creepy, chilling, and compelling, her entries into the world of the occult are simply spellbinding!" ~**Heather Graham,** *New York Times* bestselling author

"A moving mix of high suspense and romance, this haunting Halloween thriller will propel readers to bolt their doors at night." ~**Publishers Weekly** on Gingerbread Man.

CHAPTER ONE

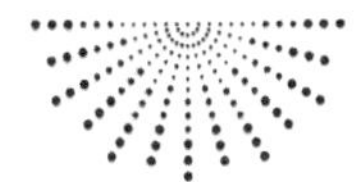

On a beautiful summer evening in upstate New York, FBI Senior Special Agent Connor "Molotov" Romano's life ended in a white-hot fireball.

He'd been heading home after another day on the job, feeling damned full of himself, too. He'd get a bonus for this one. No question. Maybe get that swimming pool Wendy had been teasing about. Or the mini-ATVs the boys had been asking for.

Thinking about his family made him remember to call home. He hit the phone button on his in-dash touchscreen, then got a little nervous when it took Wendy so long to answer. But that was the deal these days. Two kids made answering the phone fall very low on his wife's list of priorities.

She finally picked up on the third ring. "Still alive, I take it?"

He grinned. She was only half-teasing. He knew she worried every time he had a dangerous mission, and while he could never tell her the details, he always let her know the risk. That was something she'd insisted on from the start, and a concession he'd reluctantly made. She needed to be prepared for the worst, she'd said. Today had been risky. Big time risky.

"Still alive," he confirmed. "I don't think I could be this hungry otherwise."

"Stop for food, then, silly."

"Nope. In too big a hurry to get home." Brushes with death always left him with a gnawing need to hold his little boys in his arms. Four-year-old Justin and Jackson seemed to wipe out the darkness and dirt he dealt with for a living.

"The boys are in a hurry for you, too. They've been asking when you're going to be home every ten minutes for the last three hours."

"How are the little rugrats today? Drive you nuts?"

"Perfect angels like always. Jack made you a gorgeous self-portrait on the bathroom wall with a black Sharpie, and then to celebrate its completion, tried to flush a couple of pounds of Legos. Justin couldn't wait to tell on him." He laughed while she went on. "They're in the back yard now. I was just about to call them in to get cleaned up for dinner. So it went okay?"

He nodded. "Couldn't have gone better. Chalk up another win for the good guys." Today he had thwarted a plot to blow up the capital building in Albany by remotely detonating the explosives while they were still in the terrorists' van. Took out six of them in the process and really pissed off their handler, the mercenary known only as Mr. White. And not one single innocent casualty. Getting innocents killed was not an acceptable outcome to him. Never had been.

"And you're all in one piece?" Wendy asked.

"Intact. Don't worry, I'm not gonna leave you to raise our monsters alone."

She laughed softly. "How far out are you?"

"Twenty minutes."

"I'll put the lasagna into the oven. Should be ready about the time you pull in."

Wendy was a fabulous cook and a terrific mother. He loved her as much as he was capable of loving anyone. His little boys being the one exception to that. He loved them like the sun.

Their marriage hadn't been the result of any great romance, but rather the result of a potent cocktail of alcohol, libido, and carelessness. But they were making it work for the kids, and in the process they'd become best friends.

"Saw your boss today," she said. He could hear the pan sliding into the oven, the oven door closing, the soft beeps when she set the timer. "He looked guilty as hell when he saw me. Flu my ass."

"Darren? Where'd you run into him?"

"Gas station on the way to Chuck-E-Cheese for a play date. He was talking to the oddest looking—oh, hey, Justin's hanging upside down from the monkey bars and hollering at me to come out and see. Gotta go. See you when you get here."

She hung up the phone. The radio came back on. Old school Metallica filled the car, the bass booming so loud it could be heard from outside, and he stepped on it, his stomach growling in anticipation of Wendy's lasagna.

Twenty minutes later, he pulled onto their neat suburban lane, slowed down to the speed limit, and watched for kids on bikes and skateboards, and other kids walking with their eyes glued to their phone screens. Not too many outside at the moment. It wasn't quite dark. The summer sun was just getting ready to set. When his house came into sight, he smiled. It was a one-level, ranch-style haven, with a huge fenced-in yard for the boys, a back deck with a giant barbecue grill, and a basketball hoop above the garage door.

Wendy must have heard the telltale purr of his powerful engine, because she opened the front door and smiled at him, wiping her hands on a dishtowel. He waved at her, put on his signal and waited for another car to pass between him and his driveway.

And then there was a blinding flash, a deafening explosion,

and a percussion that knocked him sideways in the seat. When he lowered his arm, and came upright a rainstorm of debris was falling all around him. The shockwave had shattered the car windows. He grappled with the door and stumbled out of the car, deafened by the ringing in his ears, almost blinded from the dust cloud and debris and the blood in his eyes. He ran unevenly toward his house, his only goal getting to his family.

But the house was gone. It was just … gone.

He ran toward where it should've been, and then something fell out of the sky and flattened him to the blacktop.

The next time he opened his eyes, his boss and best friend, Assistant Director Darren Wade and his co-worker SSA and nemesis Monroe Stryker stood on either side of him. The memory of the blast shot through him like adrenalin, and he sat up in what turned out to be a hospital bed, would've jumped right out of it, if they hadn't both grabbed him by the shoulders and held him still.

"Nurse!" Darren shouted. "A little help in here!"

Stryker thumbed the call button on his bed repeatedly. Romano met Darren's eyes and saw the grief there, the message, the unspoken words. Wendy was gone. He knew that. But he had to ask all the same.

"My boys?"

Darren shook his head slowly.

An infusion of darkness filled his veins, pushing everything else out. It replaced his blood with thick, black despair. He sank back onto the bed, no longer struggling.

There was no point in getting up.

"This is White. It has to be White," Darren said.

"Does it?" Stryker's tone carried a hundred suggestions, none of them flattering.

Romano glanced at the slick, well-dressed asshole. "Yeah. Unless it was you, you bastard. Everybody knows you wanted Wendy for yourself. Did you finally get frustrated enough to do something about it?"

"I loved her, you bastard!"

"And I married her. Four years ago. You're still obsessed, though. Obsessed men do violent things."

"I'm not the explosives expert in the room."

Romano leaned out of the bed, grabbed him by the front of his shirt, and drove his knuckles into his face twice before three orderlies were pulling him off, and a nurse jabbed him with a tranquilizer. It made his brain go fuzzy before he even hit the pillows.

"I loved her," Stryker said again. "If you killed her because of that–"

"Shut the fuck up, Stryker," Darren warned. "You're out of line. Keep it up and you'll be out of a job, too. This was White. There's no question."

"Yeah? Then how the hell did White know where they lived? Huh? How did he find them with all the precautions we take to protect agents' families?"

Romano reached out with an all-but-limp hand, closed it around the I.V. pole beside him, and tried his damnedest to swing it at Stryker's head. He was unconscious before he knew whether it had connected.

CHAPTER TWO

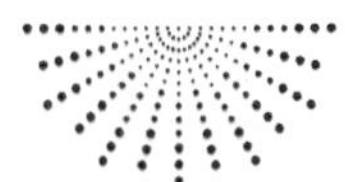

When Lexi Stoltz came home from her final day at the clinic, her genius father was in their driveway, wearing a trench coat and loading suitcases into a U-Haul van with one hand, while holding an umbrella over his head with the other.

The sun was shining and the sky was blue. It was pushing eighty degrees.

She pulled into the driveway, sighing. It was heartbreaking to watch his decline. A genius researcher whose team had created a vaccine that had nearly wiped a deadly form of malaria, he'd won a Nobel Prize for Medicine. And she was proud of him, but it was unrequited pride.

The dementia had come on suddenly, only a few weeks ago. She'd decided to quit her job at the inner-city free clinic to stay home and take care of him. They wouldn't hold her position for her, but she was a doctor, and she figured she could find another one without too much trouble when the time came.

Two weeks ago, her father had failed to come home from his job at the university for 3 days in a row. She'd gone to get him, of course, pounded on the door, begged him to just talk to her, but he'd called her an idiot and sent her packing.

That pretty much summed up their relationship. She was an unworthy admirer and he was a medical god.

Everything in her hoped this setback was something simple. She'd had elderly patients who developed symptoms like this due to a simple UTI, but so far he was adamantly refusing any doctor's appointments or medical care. So she'd brought home two weeks' worth of broad-spectrum antibiotics and a urinalysis kit. She was going to get to the bottom of this, and she would care for him herself, whether he liked it or not, the stubborn old bastard.

She drove past him into the open garage, then got out of the car, reaching back in for her purse and medical bag. But her father beat her to it, yanked her passenger door open, grabbed both bags, and hustled out to his rented van, moving as fast as a twenty-something, even if he did wobble side to side like a penguin. "Dad, what—"

He slung the bags into the back of the van, followed by the umbrella, then turned to glare at her from behind thick lenses rimmed in gold. His wild hair fit the mad-genius cliché a little too well, but she couldn't get him to sit still long enough to let her cut it.

"Get in, Lexia," he told her. "Hurry, get in. We have to go." He slammed the van doors closed and thumbed a button to close the garage door. Then he headed to the driver's side.

She hurried to keep pace. "Where are we going?" she asked.

He opened the door, but Lexi moved in front of him and blocked him from getting in. "Dad, slow down. Just tell me what's going on."

He stood still, looked into her eyes, and his were filled with impatience, anger, and no small amount of dislike. These were not new. He'd always looked at her pretty much that way. And despite the apparent confusion suggested by his actions, he was clear-eyed.

"I'm leaving," he said. "I have everything set up, and I'm leaving. Your time off begins today. You told me so, didn't you?"

"Yes, I did." She'd told him she'd resigned to care for him. She'd told him several times, and as recently as this morning. His dementia was worsening at an alarming rate. She was determined he not go into a facility. She'd keep it quiet. She wouldn't let the memory of her father be tainted by a sad and sudden decline. He was a hero. He was adored and respected the world over, by anyone who knew anything about infectious disease. His reputation was responsible for most of his team's research funding. They were making strides against multiple, deadly diseases.

She and her dad had plenty of money, and her career could wait. It was more important take care of him. To preserve his legacy.

"You're free to come with me if you want," he said. "God knows I'm going to need help, as much as it galls me to admit it. Bad enough I had to move in with you."

"Don't be ridiculous. I wanted you here."

"You can stay behind if that's what you want. I'll hire a nurse when I get there. If that's your choice, fine, but you should know that you will never see me again."

She frowned hard, a trill of alarm skittering up her spine. "Dad, what the hell is going on? What do you mean, I'll never see you again?"

He looked past her, up and down the street. "I can't tell you that. They could be listening."

God, this was far worse than she'd thought. He was completely delusional. Okay, okay, she needed to just keep him calm.

"Everything's taken care off," he said again. "The heat's turned down, and a discreet friend will check on the place once a week. I've set up timers for the lights so it'll look like we're still here. I've withdrawn a large amount of cash. Our mail will be forwarded to a service that will forward it to a lawyer who'll keep it for us to pick up. I paid top dollar. We won't be traced."

"Why would anyone want to trace us?"

"We have to go now. We have—we have to go—we have to —" He started gasping in between his words, and then he pressed one hand to his chest.

Lexi swore. "Where's your nitro, Dad?"

He reached for his pocket and missed. "Not gonna help. Have to go. House is all locked up. Everything's ... taken care of."

She dug the pill bottle from his pocket, shook out a tablet and pushed it between his lips. "I'll drive, okay? You just calm down. Don't kill yourself over this. All right?"

Panting, he nodded and shuffled around the van to the passenger side. She opened the door and helped him get in. He seemed calmer, but not enough.

She watched him buckle his seatbelt, then glanced back at the house. "Where's Jax?"

"In the back with the other boxes."

"Ah, hell, Dad." Lexi closed his door, ran around to the driver's side and got in. There was an open path to the back where it looked like everything they owned had been tossed in, some boxed, some bagged, some just loose. Shoes were scattered everywhere. A mountain, apparently made out of every outfit she owned, blocked the rear windows, and their toaster lay across the top of it.

"Jax? Kitty? Where are you, boy?"

A plaintive and far too muffled "meow" guided her to a box that was taped shut and jiggling fiercely.

Right. Her father had thrown her clothes in loose, but boxed up her cat. Rolling her eyes, Lexi peeled off the tape and her oversized goofball of a yellow cat shot out like snakes from a fake peanut can.

"Will you hurry it up, girl? I am not playing games here. We have to go, *now*."

She wasn't going to calm Jax at this point, so she let him be, and got herself into the seat behind the wheel again. "Okay, we're going." She started the van, and turned to her father. "Which way?"

"We're heading north."

She almost smiled when he said that. The only place she could think of in that direction was her mother's cabin. Well, hers now, she supposed. It was still in her mother's name, though she'd been dead for twenty-four years. She'd willed it to her daughter when she'd received her terminal diagnosis and had died before Lexi had started kindergarten. Lexi and her father hadn't been back there since.

Lexi had no idea what kind of shape the log home was in. But it was the place that held her fondest memories of her mother for her.

She backed out of the driveway and headed down the street. "How long are we staying?"

"Not very long," he told her. "Just 'til I'm dead. Now step on it, will you?"

Sighing, Lexi stepped on it.

CHAPTER THREE

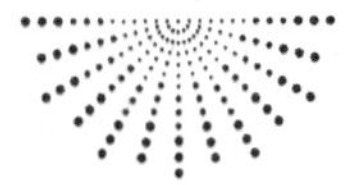

$\mathcal{D}$EA Agent Kira Waters was about to meet her half-sisters for the first time. She was nervous, which was weird, because she didn't *get* nervous anymore.

She passed a boutique, and couldn't help checking her reflection in the glass. Maybe she should've toned it down, just for today, she thought. Maybe she should've worn one of those stupid pantsuits her mother had bought her instead of leggings, over-the-knee-boots, and her signature biker jacket. But that would've clashed with the scarlet highlights in her short, dark auburn hair.

The coffee shop was just ahead. She told herself there was nothing to be nervous about as she tapped over the sidewalk, and finally through the doors out of the winter cold and into the café. She scanned the tables and spotted the women. Had to be them. Two blondes, one butterscotch, the other platinum, and a curly brunette. All three had long hair, making her self-conscious about her short cut.

The brunette glanced her way, saw her looking back, and nudged the others. They all smiled and got to their feet to greet her with awkward hugs.

"Toni Rio," said the brunette.

Her face would've been familiar even if Kira hadn't seen her picture. She was a bestselling author of true crime novels.

"You're pretty well known around the DEA, Toni. I'm gonna get a lot of mileage out of being your sister."

"And maybe I'll get a little research out of being yours?" she said, lifting her brows, making it a question.

Kira laughed it off, and turned to the platinum blonde in the pretty yellow sundress, who had the tiniest baby bump ever. "You're Cait," she said.

"I am. So good to meet you, Kira."

"You, too," she said. Toni had told her on the phone that Cait was expecting. "When are you due?"

"Not until June," Cait replied with a quick, raised-eyebrow look at the third woman, who had to be Joey.

Joey shook her head and said, "My intuition says mid-May." Then, "Great to meet you, Kira."

"You too, Joey." Kira knew about this one. In addition to talking to Toni by phone, she'd researched all of them before coming to meet them. Of course she had. She was a cop, it's what she did. Joey was a self-proclaimed psychic, and by all accounts, a pretty good one, though Kira didn't believe in that sort of thing.

They all sat down, half-sisters with the same father, who'd only recently learned of each other's existence. Kira ordered a coffee, and then there was a lot of getting-to-know-each-other chit-chat. Toni was the only one who'd been raised by the man who'd fathered them all, and Kira was full of questions about him, but about halfway through, she sensed there was something else on their minds, so she stopped talking, sipped her coffee, and looked at each of them, waiting.

Toni said, "There's one more of us. And even with my resources, we haven't been able to find her. We're hoping you might be able to help."

Kira frowned as Toni tapped her phone and handed it to her.

"She's in danger," Joey said. "I feel it right to my bones."

Kira was looking at the photo of another half-sister. She'd inherited a little more of their father's Latin blood, like Toni had, naturally brown skin and huge brown eyes. "She's beautiful," she said. "What's her name?"

"Lexia Stoltz," Toni said.

Kira's head came up fast. "*Doctor* Lexia Stoltz?"

The other three nodded.

Kira looked across at Joey. "You're right. She *is* in trouble."

"What kind of trouble?" Toni asked. She looked like she'd jump into the middle of it without much provocation, whatever it was.

"The kind I can't tell you about," Kira said. The other three looked at her expectantly, almost willing her to say more, and she looked away, then back again, and felt compelled to tell them something. "She hasn't done anything illegal or anything like that. But ... the DEA is looking for her, too. And we're not the only ones."

The genius Dr. Elliot Stoltz had died in his sleep only three weeks after they'd arrived at the massive, Adirondack log cabin. Six months after that, Lexi was still there. She'd driven the U-Haul back to pick up her car, put the house on the market, and wrapped herself up in the cabin like a big warm blanket.

Her mother had loved the place, from what she remembered. It was odd how her most vivid memories of her mom were set there. And they were happy memories; blurry, sketchy, happy memories. But they comforted her.

Lexi had only been five when her mom had died. And her father had grown steadily colder and more hateful toward her every day since. Maybe he had been before, and her mother's love had protected her from realizing it. Maybe she'd just been too young to remember.

"He's a great man, Lexi," her mother had told her. "He'll save a lot of lives. But in some ways, he's helpless too. Our job is to take care of him so he can take care of the world. In that way, we save lives, too."

She remembered that. Those words of her mother's had been repeated to her over and over. Always she'd emphasized how different her dad was, how brilliant men didn't feel emotions the way others did, and how she must never take that personally, and never let it sway her from caring for him, enabling him to do his great work.

She still didn't know what had killed her father. He'd left explicit instructions for his remains, forbidding autopsy or obituary, and requesting immediate cremation. There was nothing all that mysterious about a man of eighty-two suffering dementia or dying in his sleep. And since he'd have hated the notion of her interfering with his final wishes, she hadn't.

She'd been surprised to learn that everything he'd owned had been quietly transferred into her name a month before his death. She wondered if he'd known, somehow, that he was out of time. And she wondered why he'd given everything to her when he'd always seemed to hate her, and why he'd always seemed to hate her. Her mother had insisted he was just emotionally crippled, but it sure felt like hate to Lexi.

She wondered if coming up here to die had somehow made him feel closer to her mother, the way it did her. She wished she'd asked her questions while he was still alive.

"Who am I kidding?" she asked aloud. "He wouldn't have told me anyway."

Jax looked up at her from his spot on the rug, as close to the fireplace as he could get without singeing his yellow fur. Lexi sat in a rocker only a little bit further from the warm, yellow flames. It was good up here. Quiet. Comfortable. Serene. It was the perfect place for her to figure out what she wanted to do with the rest of her life. Odd how hard that was. Caring for her father had been her prime directive for so long, she hardly knew what to do now that he was gone.

The wind outside moaned a little louder than before, compelling her to get up and wander to the nearest window. The place had lots of windows, tall, broad ones that followed the lines of the steeply peaked cathedral ceilings in the great room. They provided a panoramic view of the snow-covered pines and the mountains all around the place. An eighteen-foot spruce tree stood in front of the tallest of them, decked in soft white lights and nothing else.

The tree farmer had sent his teenage sons up with it a week ago, lights already attached. She hadn't put another thing on the tree, and she rarely even bothered to plug it in. She kind of liked the serenity of the darkness with nothing but the orange and yellow fireplace flames to break it.

Nighttime was different up here, she thought, gazing outside. Star-spangled and natural. Alive and real. Nothing like night had been downstate. The night up here spoke in whispers, but at least it spoke.

The house tended to creak in response to the wind outside. It was as if the night moaned a question and then the house creaked an answer.

She paced away from the window, bending to stroke Jax's head when he twisted around her calves. There was nothing out there. Just forests and lakes and the speck-on-the-map town of Pine Lake a few miles down the mountain, where old men still sat around a checkerboard in the general store.

She ought to go back to bed, try to sleep, she supposed. She turned toward the curving staircase and started up it.

Then she stopped dead in her tracks and listened to what sounded absurdly like an upstairs window scraping open.

A heartbeat later, the doorbell chimed, and she almost

jumped out of her skin. No one visited her up here. Especially not in the middle of the night.

Her stomach turned queasy as she tried to decide which to investigate first. She turned toward the door, because a doorbell was certainly real, while a weird noise her brain interpreted as an upstairs window scraping open, was probably not.

Maybe it was a hunter who'd got himself lost. Or maybe one of the locals needed something. Still, there was a tingling along her nape, and her hand on the doorknob trembled a little as she turned it and pulled the door open.

The man who stood on the other side of it looked … desolate. A face of harsh angles, and eyes that held no light. Dark hair that had gone too long without a trim, and a face in need of a shave. Thick, expressive brows. Black jacket, jeans, boots.

He was looking her over just as carefully, and she shivered a little in her white flannel nightgown and bare feet.

"Can I help you?" she asked.

"I hope so." There was something about his deep, rough voice that made her nerve endings go alert and tense. "I'm looking for Dr. Elliot Stoltz."

"No one here by that name. You must have the wrong address." She had no idea what made her blurt the denial. Maybe the ghost of her father's delusional warnings before his death, that if anyone called or came by asking about him, she should deny knowing him or his whereabouts. Yes, that was part of an old man's paranoia, but the denial spilled from her lips before she had time to think better of it.

"You'll find," the dark stranger said slowly, "that it's not a real good idea to lie to me, Lexia." She blinked rapidly, drew in a shallow gasp. "That is who you are, isn't it? Dr. Lexia Stoltz?"

"Lexi Stoltz," she said. "Now it's your turn. Who are you? How do you know my name? And what are you doing at my door in the middle of the night?"

"I told you, I'm here to see your father."

Another sound came from upstairs, and it shouldn't have. A tingle of ice crept up her spine and she glanced over her shoulder toward the stairs. There was definitely something going on up there. Maybe a raccoon had got in, like in the fall.

"My father isn't here," she said. "I'm sorry you came all the way up here for nothing." She started to close the door, but he stuck a foot in the way, and her heart gave a warning flutter. "What do you think you're—"

"Sorry. I'm not buying it." He shouldered his way past her into the house. Then he took a long, slow look around as Lexi stood there watching him and trying to decide what the hell to do. She was alone. There were no landline phones and cell service was spotty at best. But he wouldn't know that.

His soulless gaze swept the room, from the flickering scented candles burning here and there, to the fireplace, to the giant spruce tree standing in the window.

"Where is he?" As he said it, he took a deliberate step toward her.

She shook her head and took an equal step away from him. "I'm calling the police. And then I'm going to turn my dogs loose, and—"

"You're not calling anyone, because there's no phone up here. And if you had dogs, they'd be barking at me by now. Listen, Lexi, I'll be a lot easier to deal with than whoever comes through that door next."

When he said that, it scared her, and the noises upstairs came back to her mind. Involuntarily, she glanced toward the wide staircase. Each step was a half log, flat side up, and the railings were birch branches and limbs still dressed in their white, knotty bark, preserved under layers of shellac. Her heart tripped over itself again and then launched into a full gallop.

"Someone's upstairs, then. Who, Lexia? Your father?"

"Stop calling me that." She averted her eyes, tried to focus on getting her heartbeat under control, but it was too late. The tachycardia was off and running.

She felt as if she wasn't getting enough air, which made her breathe more quickly, which made her dizzy. This was not an unfamiliar event, and not a dangerous one, but its timing sucked. Another sound came from upstairs then and her expression probably gave away that it shouldn't have.

The stranger—whose eyes were the darkest imaginable blue, she saw now that the firelight reached them—reached inside his coat and pulled out a handgun. When she saw it, her heart sped even faster. It felt like a jackhammer trying to break out from inside. She pressed her hands to her chest, an automatic reaction to the thundering of her heart, then spun around and ran out of the great room. She didn't even know whether she was running away from the gun or toward her stash of meds. She needed to take a pill and take it fast, before this episode got out of hand.

The beautiful Dr. Stoltz had run through a dark archway before he could stop her. Romano hadn't expected it, and something, instinct maybe, made him hesitate before going after her.

He saw where the broad staircase began, saw her stop at the base of it, and snatch a pill bottle from a stand there. She twisted it open and then quickly dry-swallowed a pill. Then she bowed her head, deliberately breathing slowly and evenly while apparently waiting for relief to come.

She stepped around the staircase, just out of his line of vision. And the second she was out of his sight, he heard her scream.

Romano ducked to one side of the doorway, peering around it, cursing his eyes for not adjusting more quickly to the dimness.

Then she came into sight again, a dark angel in a white cotton nightgown, her eyes wide with fear. But her fear had little effect on the brute who pressed a gun barrel so tight to her temple that it was probably biting into her skin. The thug, all in black and wearing a ski mask, crushed her to his chest.

There was a deep growl that drew his gaze, and then a yellow cat the size of a small mountain lion arched its back, hissed and disappeared into the depths of the place.

Romano cussed mentally, bringing his attention back where it belonged. Lexia Stoltz's eyes were rounder than ever. Dark brown, with lashes like paintbrush fringe. The guy who held her was almost invisible in the darkened room, and he apparently wasn't aware of Romano's presence. Experience and caution— or maybe instinct— had told him to park his own ride a few hundred yards down the dirt road, so they wouldn't have seen that, either.

And he had no doubt it was "they" and not just "he." Because this fellow was not Mr. White. Romano was one of the only men in US Intelligence ever to have seen White in person, if from a distance. And there was no mistaking him. This guy was one of White's henchmen, and while their boss worked alone, his muscle worked in bunches.

Romano sidled his way to the front door and slipped through it, unseen, into the winter night.

Lexi still had her pill bottle in her hand. Her heart was still running like a freight train on crack, and it would take a few minutes for the medication to kick in and convert it back to a normal rhythm.

She felt sick and dizzy, partly from fear, but mostly from the racing heartbeat. The man's grip was too tight on her, crushing her chest, which wasn't helping her tachycardia. The gun barrel pressed painfully against her temple and she was trying not to think how easily he might pull the trigger by accident.

She scanned the room for Jax. Her poor cat would be terrified by all this disruption. He was probably hiding, scared half to death.

"Where is your father?" the man rasped into her ear. When she didn't answer instantly, the gun barrel drove harder into the side of her head. "Where is he!"

He had an unusual accent. Russian, she thought. "I don't—"

"Is he here, in the house?"

"I don't know what you're—"

The barrel embedded deeper. It cut. Warm blood trickled down the side of her face. "He's not here!" She'd lost track of the stranger, but assumed that this guy was with him.

The pressure eased a little. Maybe now they'd leave, go search for her father somewhere else. What did they want with him? Why was this happening?

Someone might be after me, Lexia.

Her father's words floated back to her, as if he were speaking them now. But her father had been delusional, sick. And that was more than six months ago, almost seven, for God's sake!

The man shoved her through the archway into the great room, toward the door. She tripped over Jax and he let out a howl before streaking out of the room to hide. She stumbled on the rug but couldn't fall down. The man's grip on her was too tight to let her.

"You will take us to him, then," he said in that accent.

She'd never been so afraid in her life. And she wondered if these men meant to kill her. And where was the other one? The one who'd played good cop by knocking on the door like a human while his pal had apparently scaled her cabin and come in through an upstairs window.

"I know who you are, Lexia Stoltz," the man with the gun whispered into her ear, and his accent made his words seem even more frightening. "You will take us to your father or we will kill you. A simple choice, really. Take us to him, and we let you go."

"But my father isn't—"

The gun pressed harder. "No talk. You will take us to him."

She bit her lips to stop them from trembling. She had a feeling that no matter what she said, this animal would kill her anyway. And she couldn't have spoken a coherent phrase even if she'd wanted to, with her heart racing, and that sensation of no air. Her words were whispery at best.

Could her father have been sane all along? Was this what he'd been running away from? Had he been telling the truth when he'd told her that someone might come after him?

The man in the ski mask pulled her backward, through the front door. He stopped just outside, turning again, staring down the gravel driveway into the darkness beyond. "If you do not cooperate, it will be most unpleasant for you. And in the end, you will talk all the same. Better to do so now, and spare yourself a lot of pain."

Lexi stared into the darkness, across snowy meadows and forested hills, but there was no help for her out there. The wind was icy on her cheeks. Pine boughs sighed in time as it whispered through their needles. Early winter's chill laced the air, and it tasted like snow. It seemed like such an ordinary night. Clean and crisp and cold. She wished the cold would snap her heart back into rhythm. It might, if she could get a handful and press it to the back of her neck.

He backed down the front steps then turned to wave, and she saw a black van parked at the end of her driveway like a shark waiting there to devour her. Even the windows were tinted.

The van's headlights flashed on and it rolled closer. Ski Mask shoved her forward as the van stopped and its side door slid opened.

The interior lights came on. She planted her feet, resisting as the thug tried to shove her toward that open door. And then she saw a form crumpled on the van's floor, dressed entirely in black just like the one who held her. From inside, a booted foot nudged the body, and it rolled out and dropped to the ground.

The man holding her pushed her to down to her knees, shouting a curse, lifting his gun, and firing at the van.

The other man—the hollow-eyed stranger who'd come to her door tonight—came out of nowhere and took Ski Mask right to the ground, yanking his gun from his hand on the way, then with a bash of the butt to his skull, either knocked him out cold or killed him.

Panting, he looked up at Lexi. Her eyes never leaving his, she backed away a step, then two. He'd saved her, but for what purpose?

He bent down to pat the other man down, yanking weapons from him and shoving them into his own pockets and holsters and whatever. Then he straightened and she saw the blood on the front left side of his shirt.

It didn't matter that he'd been hurt, she told herself. He was no better than the other one, and she was getting the hell out of here.

She turned to run and wondered if she should or even could in a state of tachycardia.

"There's more of them on the way, Lexia. You won't get far."

The words were low, and she could hear the pain that laced each one. It was enough to make her pause and look back. He was pointing the gun at the ground, but he hadn't put it away. "You're either going to have to deal with me, or more like these two. Believe me, they won't be far behind."

She shook her head, shock seeping like ice water through her veins. She lifted her hands to press them to either side of her head, biting her lips to keep them from trembling. She was dizzy and her heart was still pounding far faster than it ought to.

"Dammit, get a grip. Tell me where your father is or he'll end up dead … or worse."

He was bleeding a lot. The gleaming scarlet stain on the front of his shirt grew and spread. His left arm hung useless at his side while his right one gestured with the gun as he spoke.

She took another step backward. Her car was in the garage, she thought. If she could only get to her car …

One of the men on the ground moaned, and she went still.

"Snap out of it, Lexi! Your life is in danger, or haven't you figured that out yet? You don't really want me to drive off and leave you to these two, do you?"

She dragged her eyes from the man on the ground, to the one standing in front of her. His hair was tousled and wild and his eyes were intense. His arm must be hurting. His unshaven jaw was rigid and she could see the corded muscles in his neck standing out. Yes, he was in pain. A lot of it. He came closer, lifted his wounded arm, gripped her shoulder in a hand that dripped blood. "Dammit, where is your father?"

She blinked, tearing her eyes from his to look down at one of the forms on the ground— the one that groaned again and moved a little. Then she focused on those intense eyes. In the moonlight, she saw them, pain-glazed, but piercing.

"My father is dead," she whispered, because she couldn't seem to speak louder. Fear and the tachycardia made her throat swell nearly shut.

"Dead?"

She nodded, and he swore fluently.

"All right. Okay, we'll have to search the house." His hand finally fell away from her, but she felt the sticky warmth it left behind. "Get me some rope, or duct tape or whatever you have, so I can keep these two from kicking the hell out of me. And make it fast. We have a couple of hours at most."

Lexi blinked, not moving. This wasn't happening. This couldn't be happening. My God, what did this man want? What did it have to do with her father? Why did he want to search her house?

Of all the questions swirling in her mind, she only voiced one. "A couple of hours until what?"

"Until some friends of these guys show up, or maybe some other guys who'll be just as nasty. The rope, Lexi."

"What is this all about?"

He scowled at her until his dark brows touched.

Still breathing as if she'd just run a marathon, she shook herself and turned toward the little greenhouse beside the cabin. On the way, she scooped up a handful of snow and slapped across the back of her neck. The shock it made her gasp, and there was an awful sensation in her chest as her heart converted itself back into a normal rhythm. And then it eased.

She continued on to the garden shed, the one that held all of her father's gardening tools. He used to love to putter in his garden at home, and the first thing he'd done upon arriving up here was to start a new one in the back, hoe out the old greenhouse and get it fixed up. The last three months of his life, he'd spent more time on his gardening than he'd spent with her.

Lexi hated the greenhouse.

But she went inside anyway, and she found some rope.

CHAPTER FOUR

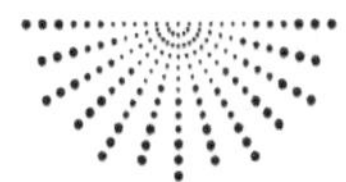

The two thugs were bound, gagged and struggling in the living room of Lexi Stoltz's log palace. Romano had blown out the candles—didn't want their thrashing around to knock one over and start a fire. He'd turned on lights, instead, half-surprised they even had lights this far up in the middle of nowhere.

Lexi didn't like the lights. She told him so without speaking a word. The way she squinted and shielded her eyes, it seemed as if she'd rather scamper off into the woods, into the dark, away from him and every ugly human being ever to draw a breath. To live out there, with her own kind, the wary woodland creatures.

The image fit. She seemed like something rarely seen by mortal eyes. Something that only came out of hiding when she was certain no one was near, afraid of being hurt or something.

She was definitely afraid of something.

The thugs most of all, at the moment. She wouldn't walk by them, even though they were tied up. But she followed Romano as he walked through the house, questioning him once or twice.

Her voice was deep and smoky. But when he passed the bad guys, she hung back.

He stopped halfway up the staircase, staring up at the seemingly endless hallway above, the countless doors lining it. "You couldn't have lived in a quaint little cottage, could you?"

His shoulder raged and nagged for attention. It was only a matter of time before more guys-in-black showed up. And here he was with a search grid the size of Grand Central.

"You're not going to get away with this, you know." She sounded like some heroine in a murder mystery. "Someone will be coming along any minute now, and you—"

"Someone will be coming along all right, but they won't be much help."

She stood just inside the archway, and though she'd been speaking to him, her eyes were glued to the two wriggling black bundles hog-tied on the floor. One of them was bleeding all over her hardwood. Her lower lip trembled. He told himself not to care.

Her wide brown eyes stayed right there in his mind's eye, though. He couldn't make them leave. Damn. There was something about her that made him want to reassure her, maybe take her by the hand and tell her it was going to be okay.

He walked away, ignored her, found her father's room and wondered if the man was really dead, or if she'd made that up. The room looked as if he'd just left it this morning. Still …

He went through drawers, closets, checked under the bed. There was a stack of papers in a shoebox under there, and he pawed through it, not finding much that stood out. A couple of unremarkable bank statements, a safe deposit box receipt, some junk mail. He shook his head, and headed back into the hallway. She was standing there waiting for him.

"Look, I don't have time to search this whole place, so I'm gonna have to trust you. Where are your father's notes?"

She blinked and her gaze finally met his. "Notes?"

"The project he was working on just before he dropped out of sight, Lexi. The biological weapon he developed. Where is it?"

Her eyes narrowed. She was either completely unaware of the mess her father had created or a very good actress. He hadn't decided which.

"My father never worked on any kind of weapon. You've got the wrong man, or the wrong information. He was a virologist."

"Yeah. That much I know."

Romano pushed a hand through his hair, rolled his eyes, swore— none of which helped the situation. When he looked at her again, she was staring at the floor near his feet. He glanced down, saw the bloodstain on the carpet, and fresh drops raining down from his arm to add to the mess.

"You're going to bleed to death." She said it matter-of-factly, as if she couldn't care less.

She had a point. He stuffed the handgun into his waistband and used his good arm to tear his shirt open. Then he shrugged out of it, balled it up and dropped it.

She gasped, which made him look at her instead of the bullet hole in his left shoulder. She was standing there with a hand pressed to her chest and it hit him that it wasn't the first time. And suddenly, her breathlessness, the paleness of her skin, made sense.

"Is it your heart? Are you—"

She avoided his touch, held up one hand. "It's fine. It's fine. It converted. Just … sore."

He blinked because he didn't know what the hell that meant. It didn't look like she was going to tell him, either. She lifted her chin, fixed her gaze on the pulsing wound in his shoulder, and took his good arm in her hand. Apparently she was no longer averse to touching him. Maybe just being touched *by* him.

Her hands were cold, but her grip was firm. She led him back up the hallway and into a white bathroom, then nodded toward a pretty little chair he wasn't sure would support his weight. He sat down anyway in front of a makeup stand or a vanity or whatever with an oval mirror. When he glanced at his own reflection, he figured it was no wonder she was afraid of him. Shirtless, bloody, his eyes as dark blue and merciless as the depths of the ocean, betraying no hint of feeling. His hair was too long. He'd abandoned the regulation cut he used to wear. He'd let it grow out during his eighteen-month attempt at retirement, since Wendy and the boys ...

Don't go there.

He pulled his focus back to his reflection. Hair, right. Too long. He hadn't bothered cutting it again for this job. It wasn't official. It was off the books. He was freelancing for one reason and one reason only. To get the man who'd murdered his family.

He heard water, saw her pouring it from a bottle onto a wad of sterile pads. She reached out and he flinched away from her. He couldn't believe it. He'd had a moment of inexplicable fear when she'd reached for him. *Him,* Molotov Romano, afraid of a skittish, colt-eyed woman.

He could have analyzed it, but he didn't. The fact was, he didn't want her touching him. He didn't need to dig into the reasons why. Rather than admit that, though, he held still while she tended his wound.

With an efficient and steady hand, Lexi Stoltz washed the blood from his shoulder and arm and chest. He inhaled and smelled her soap or shampoo as she leaned over him, and her breasts were too close to his face. So close he could see them through the white cotton nightgown.

Not a moment too soon she turned away, rummaging in a tall, freestanding cabinet and coming back with plastic bottle of alcohol and fists full of bandages, tape, and a tube of ointment. She used a syringe, sans needle, to suck alcohol from the bottle and spray it into the bullet hole, and it burned like a bastard.

"I'm surprised you didn't just let me bleed out." Maybe conversation would distract him from the pain.

"You wouldn't have bled out from this little thing."

"And yet you're patching it up."

"I'm a doctor. It's what I do." She used the syringe again, rinsing from the back this time. Then she plastered both entry and exit wounds with Neosporin and bandaged him up like a pro. "Besides, I don't want you passing out before you tell me what's going on here."

She didn't sound breathless and terrified anymore, he noticed. He didn't like her caring for his wound. And he knew why. He tried not to think of Wendy, but he thought of her anyway, and those thoughts brought searing pain with them. Wendy, small and soft and fair. She used to touch him this way, her hands gentle.

She would squeeze scented oil onto her fingers and rub it all over his back at the end of a stressful day.

Wendy. Gone now. Barely enough left of her to bury. Nothing at all left of his little boys. Their markers stood over empty graves. All because he'd failed.

He didn't have any business noticing the shape of some other woman's breasts. He closed his eyes against the pain of grief.

Lexi's hand stilled on his chest. "Did I hurt you?"

"No." His voice came out like sandpaper.

She looked at him as if she knew better. "I can get you something for the pain."

"I'm fine."

She shrugged and taped the gauze in place. "So are you going to tell me what this is all about?"

She was nearly finished. She would step away from him in a minute, put some space between them and then he'd snap out of this morbid guilt-fest.

He said, "You really don't know?"

She shook her head, her gaze pinned to his, too brown and too honest.

"Then why did you quit your job at the clinic and move up here with him?"

She shrugged. "How do you know all that?"

"It's my job to know." It wasn't. Not anymore.

She inhaled nasally, nodded as if making a decision. "My father was suffering severe dementia. The onset was sudden, the progression rapid. I resigned from the clinic to take care of him. And when he got it into his head that he had to come up here, I didn't have a choice but to come with him."

Romano had no idea the elder Dr. Stoltz hadn't been on solid mental ground. That hadn't come up in the background research he'd been given.

"I didn't know he was sick. Dementia? He got, what, forgetful, absent minded?"

"In his case, it manifested as extreme paranoia. He thought people were after him." She glanced through the open door, toward the stairs, and shuddered a little.

"Yeah, well, all due respect to your medical expertise, Doc, but that wasn't dementia."

She blinked at him. "Yeah, I was just coming to the same conclusion." Then she turned to wash her hands. But he was too astute not to notice that she only turned on the cold tap, or that she held her wrists turned up to the flow to counteract the shock. "What is it you think my father was working on? What are all you people after?"

He didn't like her lumping him in with the others, and almost said so. But he stopped himself. He didn't give a damn what she thought of him.

"He created a virus that could be weaponized, and as a weapon it would be more devastating than the A-bomb."

She shut the water off, dried her hands with a towel and met his eyes in the mirror. "He would never be involved in anything like that."

"He *was* involved in something *just* like that. He must have changed his mind right at the end. Maybe he finally understood what the repercussions could be. He took all his notes, removed the hard drives from the computers he used at the University lab and vanished from the face of the earth. Problem was, he was sloppy. He told someone."

"Who?"

He shook his head. "Don't know. But the information was leaked and now every two-bit despot and terrorist leader in the world is itching to get their hands on this thing."

Clutching the towel in her hands, she turned to face him. "And which two-bit despot or terrorist leader sent you?"

He blinked. Her voice was stronger now. Her eyes had gone as cold and hard as eyes that big and brown could get, he figured. "The good guys," he said. "Anything more than that is classified."

"Then so is anything I might know."

He rose slowly from the chair, recognizing a standoff when he saw one. He hadn't expected it. Seemed there was some toughness in her after all. Buried ... deeply buried. But there. The path to her steel lay in her old man. Say something bad about Elliot Stoltz, and arouse his daughter's anger.

"I can't tell you."

"Then you might as well leave."

He smiled just a little, knowing he had her beat. "And what do you plan to do with those two downstairs, Dr. Stoltz, or the backup crew who are probably on their way right now?"

"Nothing. I'm leaving, too. If I didn't learn another thing from my father, I learned how to disappear."

Now *that* was more in keeping with his initial impression of her. To scurry away into the woods. To burrow into a den somewhere in the forest with the other wild things.

"I found you," he told her. "They found you. They'll find you again."

"I'll run again."

"That's no way to live."

"That's my problem, isn't it?"

She was tougher than she looked. She wouldn't tell him. He could read that much in her eyes. He battled a grudging admiration for her.

"All right," he said slowly. "I'll tell you this much. The people I work for want to get their hands on this thing, but not to use as a weapon. They want it so they can develop the antidote. Once they do that, they'll make sure every trace of the virus is destroyed."

"If you believe that," she said, "then you're way too naive to be in the job you're in, whatever it is." She stepped closer, staring so deeply into his eyes that he felt her digging into his soul. "If they're going to destroy every trace of it as you claim, then why would they need an antidote?"

"Just in case they missed something. A note, a vial, a sample."

She stared at him so hard it felt like she was trying to see inside him, maybe trying to decide whether he could be trusted.

"Look, I've got one goal. To stop this weapon from falling into the hands of someone like Putin or Kim Jong Il or the effing Saudis."

"How do I know I can believe you?"

"You don't."

She stood there a moment, deep in thought. Finally she shook her head. "It's all a mistake, anyway. There is no killer virus. My father was a great man. His work has saved countless lives. He would never create something like that."

"He not only would, he did."

"No, he didn't. I'll never believe it. He would have told me." She let her voice trail off, uncertainty clouding her eyes.

"Would he?"

Her chin came up, and her gaze met his. "He couldn't have done what you say he did."

"Okay. I say he did it, and you say he didn't. There's only one way to prove which of us is right."

She closed her eyes, clenched jaw. "I have to process this. I need time to think—"

"There *is* no time to think, Doc. I'm not lying when I say more men like those two downstairs will be showing up soon. And they'll do everything they said they'd do to you and then some."

Her eyes opened and she faced him. He thought maybe she'd come to a decision.

"My father didn't work the entire time we were here. He didn't bring a computer. Nothing from the lab. There's nothing here."

He found he could read her like a book. Her expressions were transparent. And he believed her. "There was a safe deposit box receipt in his papers. Could there be anything there?"

"If there were anything to find, it would more likely be there than here." She averted her eyes a little bit.

He nodded slowly. "You're sure there are no notes here in the house?"

"I'm sure." He turned her chin so he could watch her face as she spoke. She frowned, but met his gaze head on. "I went through everything after he passed. There were no research notes, no formulae, nothing like that."

Just a mystery safe deposit box. It wasn't much, but it was something. "I want the name of the bank. And then I want the key."

She frowned as if searching her mind again. Then she turned and left the room. Romano followed her down the hall, into a bedroom that had to be hers. The rumpled bed, the cat peering out from underneath it. She yanked open a dresser drawer, took out a pair of jeans and bent to step into them, tugging them on under the nightgown, snapping, zipping, and making him feel a stir he had no business feeling.

"What the hell are you doing?"

"Getting dressed. I'll give you the key and then I'm leaving. All right?" She didn't wait for an answer. She dug through the dresser again, emerging this time with a shirt. Turning her back, she tugged the nightgown off over her head.

Romano stood like his feet had grown roots, staring at the length of her bare arms, the curve of her spine, the soft, smooth roundness of her shoulders.

With great effort, he averted his eyes and tried to focus on something else besides her. The fireplace on one wall, not burning. The neat stack of kindling and wood on the grate, ready for the touch of a match. The brass log holder, filled with fragrant, seasoned cherry wood.

"You'll leave me alone?" she asked. "You promise? If there's anything to be found, it will be in that safe deposit box. And whatever you do find, it's only going to prove that you're wrong."

He looked at her again. She was buttoning the pretty white blouse. Thank God for small favors.

He went silent at the sound of tires crunching gravel, cussed himself for not grabbing that receipt from the old man's room. First National Bank, New York, New York, that much he remembered. Which branch? What was the box number?

He looked to the hall, wondering if he could dash back down to her father's room and grab that receipt. "We're out of time," he said in answer to his own internal question.

She looked up quickly, and all her courage dissolved before his eyes. Her fear returned. "You're coming with me, you understand? If you want to survive this, don't argue about it. Now get the damned key and let's get out of here."

She looked defeated. Like he'd just let all the air out of her balloon. it would have been laughable if the situation hadn't been so deadly. Turning, she dumped a jewelry box onto her dresser, pawing through a small mountain of trinkets. He saw the key as she dug it out of the mess, and before he'd even extended his hand for it, she'd tucked it into her jeans pocket.

The sound of doors slamming on the vehicle out front came loud and clear. "Oh, God," she whispered. But she never stopped moving. She swooped down on a pair of sneakers that had been hiding under the bed, stuffed her feet into them. She was shaking again, breathing hard. She snatched the pill bottle from the dresser where she'd dropped it, crammed it into a handbag that she clutched it in a white-knuckled grip.

"Is there a back door?" Romano whispered harshly.

"We'd have to go back downstairs."

He lunged for the window, shoved it open and stuck his head out. "No fire escape? Nothing?"

"How many log cabins have you seen with fire escapes attached?" She looked terrified when the front door opened audibly below. Then she blinked. "There are rope ladders in every bedroom." She opened the closet and hauled a flimsy-looking rope ladder from an upper shelf.

Romano took the bundle from her, anchored the two end hooks on the window ledge and let the rest fall free.

"Come on," he whispered harshly. "Hurry. Get out there."

"I don't want to leave my cat!"

"You'll leave him on angel wings with a harp in your hands if you don't get your ass in gear!"

She sent a desperate glance toward the bed, where the cat had been only seconds ago, but the beast had gone into hiding. She shook her head, staring at the open window, then at him.

Romano heard heavy footfalls on the stairs. Lexi bit her lip and awkwardly, she climbed through the window and made her way down the ladder.

It was not Lexi Stoltz climbing down that rope ladder in the middle of the night while killers invaded her home. The woman she'd believed herself to be would have been hiding under the bed with Jax.

But something had happened to her up there, something she hadn't been aware *could* happen. She'd suddenly stepped out of herself, and stood calmly, watching events unfold like she was watching a scary movie. And something else had taken over. Something stronger and braver than she'd ever believed lived in her. She didn't recognize that thing. It was like an alien presence, summoned to life by a strong pair of hands gripping her shoulders, and by blue-black eyes boring into hers. The confident, capable, kick-ass-and-take-names stranger had roused some new, unfamiliar part of her to life. She didn't know how, but she was grateful enough that she almost felt guilty for lying to him about the safe-deposit box.

Oh, it had existed, once. When he'd asked about it, it had seemed like a gift—a distraction to toss his way just to get him to leave.

But then those others had arrived, and she'd realized she needed him to keep her alive.

The key in her pocket went to her PO Box in nearby Pine Lake. If he got a close look at it, he'd know that.

She just needed to get him out of here, and then find an opportunity to ditch him. She'd come back just long enough to grab Jax, and then she'd find somewhere safe to hole up while she dug into this nonsense and found the truth.

She needed to prove her father hadn't done what he was accused of. God, if she'd been worried about what extreme end-of-life dementia would do to his legacy, what would this do to it?

Not to mention, to all his other work. Vital work. And to the university and to his team! And to all the victims of viruses who wouldn't be protected if her father's work came to a grinding halt.

She stood on the ground below her bedroom window, watching the man descend. She could hear the others, inside, shouting and moving through the place, and she felt no further hint of that brave woman she'd temporarily become.

The stranger jumped when he was still ten feet from the ground, rolled to his feet, gripped her arm and pulled her into the snowy pine forest beyond her back lawn.

She wished for boots. For a coat. For a hat. It was freezing outside.

He seemed to know where he was going, and that gave her a little confidence. Getting lost in the vast Adirondack preserve was a terrifying prospect.

He veered westward, cutting a diagonal path through the woods that would bring them around to the only road. She had to struggle to keep the pace he set, but at least the snow wasn't as deep here where the pine boughs interlocked to form a canopy. Wintry night air rushed in and out of her lungs. She kept looking back over her shoulder as they ran, expecting to see an army of thugs chasing them. But there were none in sight. Not yet, anyway. They'd know where to look for them, though. The rope ladder was still hanging from the window.

Maybe Jax would find it and use it to escape. Or maybe he'd stay hidden until those men left. The poor thing.

Finally, he stopped at the edge of the woods near the winding dirt road. He wasn't even winded, though Lexi panted like a racehorse and hoped no one could hear. She sank to the ground and its cushion of pine needles, watching him stare out at the road. Her heart was racing again, and she automatically pulled her pills from her purse and took another one. Two were okay. More than that, not so much.

He tilted his head, listening.

Then he turned to her and jerked his head. She rose, though

she wanted to stay right where she was. He led her out onto the road. A car sat a few yards away, and that was where he took her, moving fast and silent. She tried to be as quiet as he was, but wasn't having much success. He stopped beside the car, slipping a penlight from a pocket. Then he was on his belly, shining the light underneath. He got up, checked the car's interior and opened the driver's door. "Get in."

"But—"

"Hurry, Lexi. The keys are in the switch. Don't start the engine yet. There's a phone in the console."

"There's no signal—"

"Use it to mark time. When five minutes have passed, start the car. Wait two more minutes. If I'm not back by then, get the hell out of here."

"Where are you going?"

"No time. Just do what I said, okay?"

"I don't think I can—"

"You'll be fine. Just give me those two counts to get back. Don't ditch me, or I'll be dead. Okay?"

She nodded, sliding into the driver's seat. He opened the trunk, took out a small satchel. Then he closed it without making a sound, turned and ran into the woods.

She slid her damp palms back and forth over the steering wheel as she dug around in the console for his cell phone. Its background image brought her up short. Two little boys posing in front of a decked-out Christmas tree.

This man definitely didn't seem like daddy-material. They were probably nephews or something.

She sat there, watching the area around her, waiting, keeping track of the time. She spotted movement in the trees, then realized it was just the pine limbs swaying lazily in the wind.

His car was a Porsche with an aggressive, snarling grill. Jet black, inside and out. Expensive. It smelled new.

The digits changed. Five minutes had passed. She prayed the

bad guys had all gone deaf, depressed the clutch and started the car. It growled to life, then sat purring like Jax after a big meal. She stared at the phone, adjusted the mirror so she could see behind her. She checked the emergency brake. It was on, so she released it. As the clock ticked another minute away, she slid the shift into first gear and tried to remember the last time she'd driven a stick.

Why was she even waiting for him? Why didn't she just leave? She had his car, she had his keys, she had his phone. She could get away.

Don't ditch me or I'll be dead.

She closed her eyes and told herself she wasn't waiting one second longer than those two minutes.

The passenger door flew open and he dove in, tossing his satchel into the back. She was so startled her foot slipped off the clutch and the car stalled.

He swore. "Come on, Lexi! Go!"

She started the car, released the brake and managed to take off this time, quickly shifting into second, then third. "Are they following us?" she asked, looking up at the mirror.

"Shift! Come on!"

She shifted into fourth gear, negotiated a curve, picked up speed and shifted again. Behind her she could only see the snowy rooster-tail thrown up by the car's tires. Ahead, only darkness. She reached for the headlight switch. He covered her hand.

"Not yet."

"I can't drive at this speed in the dark!" She'd get them both killed if she tried to go any faster. "Are they—"

"Yeah, they're coming."

Her foot pressed harder on the accelerator. "This is insane. I'm running for my life in the middle of the night with a total stranger. I can't drive this car! I've never driven a car like this in my life!"

"Wouldn't have known that. You're kicking ass. Go faster."

"God, I don't even know your name!"

"Romano," he said.

She glanced at him briefly, not daring to take her eyes from the barely visible road ahead for more than an instant. He was turned in his seat, staring behind them, and he held something in his hand that she couldn't identify. Not a gun.

"Romano?" she repeated stupidly.

"Molotov to my friends."

"Molotov?" She swung the wheel and the car veered wildly. She'd almost missed that curve. "Why Molotov?"

His answer was a slow grin, and he lifted the thing he held, pointing it behind them and pressing a button with his thumb.

An explosion rocked the earth. The car vibrated with it. The night glowed for a moment, and Lexi jammed the brake and the clutch at the same time, skidding to a stop.

She looked behind them, saw what had been that another dark van, minus several important parts. A bumper landed right behind the Porsche and she jumped so hard her head bumped the ceiling.

The van was on fire and men were spilling out of it like cockroaches when the lights come on. They scurried, then regrouped and ran forward, and she heard a rat-a-tat sound she couldn't place at first.

Then the back window exploded, and she screamed.

The man who called himself Molotov—for obvious reasons —gripped her waist in his large hands and pulled her onto his lap. Before she could yell again, he was sliding out from beneath her into the driver's seat. In what seemed like a heartbeat, they were flying, and one of his hands rose to the back of her head.

"Stay down, Lexi."

Lexi stayed down.

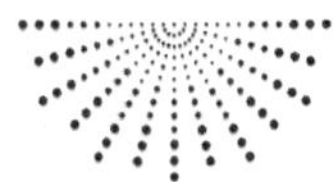

*R*omano didn't know where her brief flash of moxie had come from, but it was gone now. She was curled into the passenger seat, hugging her knees to her chest, her long sable hair hiding her face. And he thought she was crying. Trembling, too.

When they finally hit a paved road, he slowed down just enough to avoid drawing undue attention. He turned up the heat, but it still didn't make up for the winter cold coming through the demolished back window. She must be freezing, as well as terrified. Not to mention sick. He didn't know much about those short of breath, chest grasping moments she'd had back there, but he didn't imagine being traumatized and half frozen was exactly good for them. He wished she'd speak, strike up a conversation, say something, anything, but he didn't expect her to. He wanted to draw her out of her shell and told himself that was just because it would make their forced companionship a little less awkward and tense.

"Are you sick or something?" he asked.

"No."

One word answers. Great. "Is it asthma?" He didn't know

why the hell he'd asked that. He didn't want to know anything about Lexia Stoltz, except where her father had hidden his man-made disease. He didn't care about her health, that was for damn sure.

"PSVT."

"I don't know what that is." Let her answer that with one word, he thought.

"Paroxysmal Supraventricular Tachycardia."

Three words. None of them in any language he spoke, except that last one. Tachycardia.

"That means it's something with your heart, right?"

"It sounds scarier than it is."

"Looks scarier than it is, too, I hope?"

She lifted her head a little, so her hair fell back and revealed her face, as she glanced sideways at him.

He shrugged. "When you grabbed your chest back there, it shook me."

She looked at him a minute, like she was trying to see if he meant it. Then she said, "It's like a misfiring spark plug. An electrical signal gets garbled, and tells my heart rate to go up too high. I didn't count, but this was a really good one. Probably around two-twenty."

"Two *hundred* twenty? Per minute?" He shot her a look, and he thought his own heart was speeding up a little. "That's almost four beats a second."

She nodded. "When it happens, I feel like I can't breathe, even though I can. My blood isn't carrying oxygen efficiently, so my respirations automatically get faster to try to make up for it. I get dizzy. I feel weak. Simple hyperventilation, but knowing it doesn't help all that much. The worst that can happen is that I pass out. But it's not damaging my heart muscle or anything, and if I take a simple beta blocker, it'll convert back to a normal rhythm within a few minutes."

"A few minutes seems like a long time to spend in that condition. What if you don't have a … beta blocker on hand?"

"Don't worry. I brought them."

"Yeah, but what if you hadn't? Or what if you have an episode and I can't get to the meds for some reason?"

She frowned at him. "You worried about me? That's kind of funny, seeing as how you've basically kidnapped me."

"I rescued you. You'd be undergoing torture right now if I hadn't— shit that was a stupid thing to say." He glanced at her, trying to see if his idiotic words had triggered another episode, but she just rolled her eyes at him as if she knew. "Just tell me," he said. "I'll feel better."

"God knows making you feeling better is my *raison d'être.*"

"Just tell me." He liked that she'd snapped at him. It made him more confident in her ability to handle all this.

"If I don't have a pill, I can usually convert myself. Methods that work are bearing down. If that doesn't work, I slap an icepack on the back of my neck or the middle of my lower back, anyplace that it's going to shock me with the cold. It's the shock that helps. And then if all else fails, I can perform carotid massage, kind of squeezing off the blood supply to my brain for a couple of seconds. That usually does the trick."

"That sounds horrible."

"It's not that bad. The episodes can be exhausting. And converting back to normal rhythm is scary, because I can feel it. There's always a really severe tightening and pain in my heart, just for a second, like someone's reaching inside and squeezing it with all their might. And then a little, thump-a-thump, and it's back to beating normally again."

"Isn't there any way to fix it?"

"There's a surgery. But I only have a couple of episodes a year. To me, that's too little to justify letting a surgeon go digging around in my heart."

"Amen to that."

Sighing, she leaned back in her seat. He sensed her closing up again, like a flower when the sun goes down. He wanted to keep her talking. "Have you had it long?"

"Since my teens. It used to drive my father crazy, having to take time off work to run me to doctors and hospitals before we had a firm diagnosis."

Romano noticed her hands clasping each other more tightly as she spoke. Her father sounded like a real piece of work. "So, stress brings it on?"

She shrugged, opening her eyes again, even looking at him for a second. "It's one trigger. There are others. I've had it just happen in my sleep so …"

"Before I came, when was the last one?"

She closed her eyes. "The morning I found my father in his bed."

Romano found himself envisioning her, alone in that over-sized log cabin, finding her father that way. According to the information he'd been provided, she'd adored the man.

"I'm really sorry I brought that up," he said.

"It doesn't matter."

At least she was talking. When she talked, he could focus on her words, her tone. He could hear more than people said, picking up on inflections and shifts in volume and air to sound ratio. He'd always been able to do that. It had made him a better agent. Of course it wasn't 100% accurate, but he considered it his superpower and he trusted it.

When she went silent, it was easy to start searching her eyes and imagining he could read every emotion in them. Way too easy.

Stress-induced, she'd said. Well, then, it was no wonder she'd had an attack. She'd certainly had some stress in the past few hours. But it couldn't be helped. He had to get the formula, and he had to find, identify, and kill the international criminal known as Mr. White. Lexi and her heart be damned.

"So where is this safe-deposit box located, Lexi?" He asked just to see if she'd tell the truth, because he'd felt something off about that.

"New York."

He nodded. "Right, right, I saw that. First National, right?"

She nodded.

"Which branch?"

"You didn't see that on the receipt you found?"

"No."

She took a few steadying breaths. He figured she was calling on the hidden reserve of strength she kept locked away somewhere inside her. He wondered if she'd stumbled onto it by accident when he'd caught a glimpse of it before, or whether she'd always known it was there.

Her eyes were trying to be strong, but there was fear behind them. "If you're done rescuing me, I think it's safe to let me go now. Okay?"

"I don't think so."

"You don't need me. I'll tell you which branch and give you the key, but only if you let me go."

Her tone was unsteady, her breathing had a hitch in it. He studied her in short glances while driving. Damned if she wasn't up to something. He could read her like a book. "I thought you'd *want* to go with me. Seems like you'd want to see what I find in that box for yourself, especially since you're so sure it'll prove your old man innocent."

"Whatever you eventually find is going to do that."

"So how do you know I can be trusted to report what's really in there? How do you know I won't lie and ruin his impeccable name, no matter what I find?"

"What would you have to gain by doing that?" she asked.

He glanced at her, shrugged. "If I had something to gain by it, I wouldn't tell you what it was." He had to be careful with her. She was smart. Maybe smarter than him.

Definitely smarter than him.

She bit her lip, shook her head. "I'm just not cut out for this."

"No, most people aren't." He sighed hard, almost regretting that he was about to drag her with him into hell. But he didn't have a choice.

"Look, Lexi, if I let you go, those guys will track you down. It won't matter where you go or how well you think you can hide. Sooner or later, they'll find you, and try to force you to tell them what they want to know. They're not going to believe you don't know anything. And even if you somehow managed to convince them, they'd kill you anyway."

She shook her head. "No one's that brutal."

"Trust me. I know *exactly* how brutal they are."

"You've dealt with them before?"

Her eyes took on a new look, a curious one. He clamped his jaw, deliberately not looking at her. He didn't want her digging into his mind, much less probing his pain. He needed his pain. Wendy, Justin and Jackson deserved his pain. And Lexi's brown eyes might be powerful enough to see right into the black, bottomless pit of his grief. She'd look into the empty socket where his soul used to live. It was gone now. It had died with his little boys.

"You're not gonna be safe until I get that formula to my boss. I'll let you go then. Until that point, you're stuck with me." He glanced her way. "Now, how about handing over that key?"

She shook her head.

He sent her his meanest glare, but it was ineffective since she refused to look him in the eye. "How about telling me which branch, then?"

"I'll tell you when we get to the city."

"Care to explain your reasons?"

Her white teeth worried her lower lip for a moment. "I've already told you, my father couldn't have done this." She drew a shaky breath. "And … even if he did stumble onto some potential biological weapon, then he did it by accident."

"I don't really care if it was deliberate or not. Your father created a monster, and then he took it and ran."

"Maybe he wished he hadn't found it at all," she said. "You said he deleted his files, took all his notes."

"So?"

"So, if this thing ever existed, he would have destroyed it himself."

"You're dead wrong about that."

She tilted her head, staring at him, tears slowly drying on her lashes. "I know my father."

"I know his type."

"You don't know anything about him at all," she said, but softly. Her tone lacked conviction.

"Lexi, this was probably the most important breakthrough of your father's entire career. Do you really think he'd just destroy every trace of it?" She blinked at him, apparently unable to look away. "I don't," he went on. "I think he had enough ego that he'd have to keep some part of it, the formula, a tiny sample, a cryptic note, something."

Her knees lowered until her feet rested on the floor. She tipped her head back, resting it on the seat behind her. "You're wrong. You … have to be wrong."

"Sure I am. And you're so loyal to him because … what, he was the world's most wonderful father?"

She flinched in genuine pain, intense enough that it brought tears to her eyes. He'd touched a raw spot. "He was a great man. His work has saved countless lives."

"Yeah, got it. Well, listen, we can't take a chance that you're the one who's wrong about him. We have to be sure. The guys at your house are mercenaries. The monster who hired them will do anything to get his hands on this. And then he'll sell it to the highest bidder."

"And I'm supposed to trust that you don't plan to do the same thing? On the off chance that there is actually anything to sell."

"There's no way for me to prove myself to you, and I don't really have time. Trust me or don't. Either way, we're doing this."

She closed her eyes, sighed long and hard. "I'm not giving you the key or telling you which branch."

"Cause you think I'm in it for the money."

"Because I think you won't murder me until I do."

Those words were an arrow that stabbed him hard, and unexpectedly. What the hell did he care if she didn't trust him? It was nothing to him. *She* was nothing to him. A means to an end, that end being Mr. White.

"I'm going to prove you wrong," Lexi said. "I'm not going to let you destroy my father's life's work, work that's going on, even today, funded in large part because of his reputation. I will not let you leave a black mark on his life story. He was a genius. He was a scientist. He contributed more to society than you or I could ever hope to do. I'm going to fix this. I'm going to do what my mother would have expected me to do. Protect him."

Romano had the feeling she was speaking more to herself than to him. He sensed it was important, what she'd just said, and started wondering about her relationship with her sainted father.

No way, Romano. Leave it lie. You don't give a damn about her, remember?

"You're not gonna like what you find," he told her. "Prepare yourself for that."

"I've got to protect his legacy."

Admiration welled up in his throat. She had backbone, and she had a good heart. He was pretty sure her loyalty to her old man was sorely misplaced, but it was sure as hell solid.

"You might need a refill on that medicine of yours before this is over." He gunned the gas and the car shot forward.

"Molotov" Romano came out of the motel office with one key dangling from his good hand, and Lexi couldn't take her eyes off him as he crossed the parking lot toward the car, where she waited.

She wasn't sure why she hadn't run away. She'd thought about it. But it didn't seem like she'd get very far if she tried. It wasn't the right time, not yet.

Her hero-captor wore a denim jacket that had been lying in the back seat. His black one had been left behind in her house, bloody and with a bullet hole in the front. He'd have attracted too much attention, walking in shirtless with a bandaged-up shoulder.

He'd have attracted too much attention just with the shirt-less part. The guy was cut. And scarred to hell and gone. He looked like he was carrying around a message in runic, carved into his flesh in the form of scars.

As he strode purposefully toward her, jacket hanging open, bare, scarred-up, muscular chest there for all to see, she figured he'd attracted attention anyway.

Not hers, though. To her, he looked scary. He was too big and too hard. A little bit too virile. She'd prefer an intellectual man, one who was all brain and little brawn. She'd prefer a man with short, tame hair. Not the wild waves that suggested a stallion's mane. She'd prefer a man who was shy and sensitive, and who didn't keep his feelings to himself, the way this one did.

When she looked into his eyes, she saw darkness. It was bleak in his soul, and she couldn't help but wonder why.

He looked tough, she mused. Like someone you wouldn't

want to cross, or even look at wrong. She could never be attracted to a man as ominous and unapproachable as he was.

He got into the car without looking at her, and drove it around behind the motel, parking between a camper and a pickup truck. She wondered why, when there were a dozen empty spots with a lot more room. And then she realized it was to keep the car out of sight. Maybe he thought the bad guys had seen it. He seemed to think of everything, this guy. He might be muscular, but he was smart, too.

Who did he work for? What kind of man did this kind of thing for a living? If she'd thought of spies and action heroes at all, she'd thought they only existed in the movies. But this was real and she was swept up in it.

It didn't matter, she told herself. She wouldn't be with him much longer.

She didn't trust him. And she didn't want him getting a close look at that key until she was ready to run.

But now wasn't the time. He was faster than her, stronger. Just bolting in the middle of nowhere wasn't an option. He'd chase her down in short order. She had to be smarter than him. Give herself time to put distance between them. So she was going to slip away while he was sleeping. He had to sleep, didn't he?

She'd been thinking, and realized that she'd spent her whole life taking care of her father, forgiving him for not caring for her in return, excusing him because of his greatness, and waiting the entire time for his approval. And he'd died without giving it. Not once. She wasn't a gullible child anymore. She knew there were great men who loved. He just wasn't one of them.

If she could just do this one last thing, if she could save the legacy that had meant so much to so many, then she would have fulfilled her mother's wishes. And somehow she thought she'd be able to let go, after that. She could stop existing all curled up inside herself, and get up and stretch and step outside. She could start living again.

Outsmarting Romano, though, was going to be challenging.

"Our room awaits," he announced as he got out.

She stopped shivering, crossed her arms over her chest. "What do you mean, *our* room?"

He didn't stop walking. Just paused in front of a door, inserted the key and opened it with a flourish. "I don't trust you any more than you trust me, Lexi. Wouldn't surprise me if you were planning to take the key and go to the bank alone. In which case you'd get killed, Mr. White would get the formula, and the maniacal world leader with the most cash on hand would use it to wipe out countless people. What happens once a virus is set loose on the world, Dr. Stoltz?"

She blinked slowly, getting out of the car and going to the door as he unlocked it. "Under the right conditions, it would multiply. Reproduce. Continue to mutate."

"Exactly. And I'd lose my chance to get ..." He came to an awkward stop, shifted his eyes to hers and said, "Paid. And it's gonna be a big check. Biggest one ever."

So he was only in this for the money. She didn't know why she was disappointed, but she was. Bitterly.

Well, he'd guessed right. She *was* leaving. And she'd be heading in the opposite direction of the city, where both sets of her pursuers would expect her to be going.

It would have been easier with separate rooms. Maybe she could talk him into it.

"I'm not sleeping with you." She blurted the sentence before fully composing it in her mind. "I mean, I'm not—"

"Two beds, Lexi. I promise to stay in mine if you promise to stay in yours. Okay?"

"No, it's not okay."

"Well, if you're afraid you won't be *able* to stay in yours, that's okay, too. I mean, I'm as red-blooded as the next guy—"

He broke off when her hand came flying up. She froze just before her palm connected with his face, and she stared at her hand, blinking in shock. My God, she'd almost slapped him. That wasn't like her. It wasn't *anything* like her. What was happening to her?

And what in the world was the matter with *him?* He hadn't flinched, hadn't drawn back, hadn't tried to stop her.

"Chicken," he said.

"What?"

"Nothing. I rented one room. I'm not renting another one. Deal with it."

He held the door open, waved her inside, and she went in. She was too tired to argue with him. He came in behind her, closed the door and locked it. Then he tossed the key onto the nearest bed, followed by his jacket. Then he laid down beside his stuff, face up. "I could use a nap."

"Yeah, except I'm starving and dehydrated. Even prisoners get bread and water."

"Nag, nag, nag."

She almost smiled, just caught it in time.

"Well? Come on, I said nag. Go ahead. Let me have it."

She closed her eyes, shook her head. She didn't understand this guy at all. "Fine. You drag me out of my home, without even a chance to pack—"

"There were killers coming up the stairs at the time."

"I had to leave my poor cat. And who knows what those maniacs have done to Jax by now?"

"I'm sorry about the cat. I tried to get him before I came down the rope ladder. Reached under the bed for him, but—" there he held up his forearm, and she saw three long scratches she hadn't noticed before.

"Jax did that?"

He nodded. "The bedroom door was still open a crack, and he shot through it before I could grab him." He sighed, lowered his arm again. "He'll crawl under something and hide until it's quiet. He's a cat, they have a sixth sense about people."

He was trying to comfort her, she thought. "I think they say that about dogs."

"Back to your rant? I don't think you were done, were you?"

"No. I'm tired. I'm hungry and thirsty and I need a shower. I know I can take one. but I don't even have clean clothes to put on, and this all just … frankly, it sucks."

"There. Feel better?"

She glared at him.

He got up and went back out to the car without another word, leaving the door open behind him. She watched his broad back and wished to God he'd put on a shirt at some point in the near future. He opened the trunk, and when he closed it again, he had a duffel bag over his shoulder.

Once back inside, he dropped the bag onto the bed she'd decided must be hers.

"There you go. Knock yourself out."

"You have food in there?"

"A banquet. And help yourself to the clothes." He was on the bed again, but he lifted his head to look her up and down. "They'll be big, but I imagine you'd look good in a feed bag."

Had he just complimented her? Too late to tell, he'd closed his eyes. His chest rose and fell slowly, expanding and then collapsing again in a steady rhythm. The sounds of his breaths almost hypnotized her.

What kind of an idiot was she, anyway?

She loosened the drawstring on the duffel and tried not to ignore the mesmerizing music he was making. It wasn't easy.

The bag was crammed full of stuff. Maybe she could learn something about the mysterious man who called himself Molotov if she looked through his worldly possessions.

"Food's in that pocket on the front. And there oughtta be a T-shirt right on top."

She jumped a foot. He smiled without opening his eyes.

Fishing out a T-shirt, she took it with her into the bathroom and locked the door behind her. But even locked away from him in the small bathroom, she couldn't get him out of her mind. Obviously, he didn't want her looking through the duffel bag. Which meant he had something to hide. Not that she cared. Not that it mattered what secrets he was keeping. She had her own plan, and it might be the most important one of her life.

So she showered, taking her sweet time about it. And when she finished, she put her clothes back on, ignoring the oversized black T-shirt she'd borrowed. And then she cracked the door.

He was snoring softly and after a full minute watching him, she was sure he was asleep. All right then. This was the chance she'd been waiting for, and it might be the only one she'd get. She crossed the room in her sock feet, not making so much as a sound. Bending to grab her sneakers and purse as she passed them, utterly silent, she approached the door, but her eyes were on him.

Romano never moved, just kept snoring, sleeping. His eyelashes seemed thicker and darker now than when he was awake. Or was it just the way they contrasted against his cheeks? They gave him a little boy look that vanished as soon as he opened them to reveal the stone-cold irises they covered.

She stopped at the door, her hand on the knob.

"Taking a midnight stroll, Lexi?"

"Just … checking the lock."

"You need your shoes and bag for that?"

She dropped the shoes to the floor, shook her head in self-disgust. "I thought I was silent as a cat."

Romano sat up in bed, so the covers fell down to his hips, baring his chest, which was making her feel wrong in so many ways she couldn't count them all. "You were pretty quiet. But

I'm the world's lightest sleeper." His midnight blue eyes were amused, not angry. And they were in constant motion, those eyes. He didn't just look at her face, but took in the whole of her, head to toe, again and again.

"Get some sleep, Lexi. You'll need it."

"I don't think I could sleep if I tried."

He swung his legs over the side of the bed with a sigh. "Then maybe you can help me solve a problem." Leaning forward, he pulled a pair of jeans out of the duffel, dropped them on the bed. She watched him like a hawk. Her eyes were a little bit too interested in the way the muscles in his back and shoulders moved beneath the skin. And the way his dark hair fell over his neck, curling a little at the ends.

There was a strength about him, and she sensed it went deeper than just the physical aspects.

"What problem?" She wished to hell he'd put a shirt on.

He turned toward her, the duffel dangling from his right arm. Its weight made his biceps bulge, and for a second she couldn't look away. Then she forced her gaze elsewhere and wound up looking at his abs. What was the matter with her? Hadn't she ever seen a man with a decent bod before?

Yeah, she had, up close. She was a doctor; there was no body type she hadn't seen.

"The problem," he said, "is how the hell I can take a shower without you sneaking out of here and getting yourself dead."

"I'll stay. I promise." Her voice was kind of raspy.

"You're a terrible liar. Really bad. Listen, you wouldn't get far. I'll come after you, naked and wet if necessary, throw you over my shoulder and haul your ass back here. You can't outrun me."

She tried not to imagine him naked and wet and hauling her back to the motel room like some kind of caveman. And imagined it anyway. "I'll stay."

"You'd better." He turned his attention back to the bag,

pulled out another black T-shirt. As he did, a small, three-by-five photo frame clattered to the to the floor. It landed and she had a perfectly clear view of it in the light spilling into the room from outside.

She looked from the faces in that photo to him again. The hard, cold coating his eyes usually wore melted like ice under a blazing sun, revealing what it usually hid. Pain. Stark, intense pain.

Since he didn't move, she did, stepping forward and dropping to her haunches. The photo was of a cool, elegant blonde and two little boys, one a toddler, one a little older. The boys could've been Romano's miniatures, except that their deep blue eyes sparkled with mischief and joy, and their black hair was curlier than his. They were the same two kids she'd seen on his phone.

She looked up at him, tried to imagine him as a family man, a man with a pretty wife and adorable little boys, but it was hard to fit him into that scenario. It didn't compute.

She reached for the photo, then jerked backward when he snatched it up before she could.

She caught his gaze again and saw an aching and vulnerable man battling demons only he could see. His shoulders bowed just slightly, his chin was angled lower, his jaw had softened.

Then he turned himself so he was facing away from her and put the photo into one of the duffel's side pockets.

"Who are they?"

He said nothing. Just dropped the bag onto the bed, and kept his face averted.

Something about his pain got to her. She could've predicted it. She was a nurturer, a healer. She liked taking care of people, probably because it made her feel needed. Prior to her career in medicine, no one had ever needed her. Well, except for Jax.

She missed that lazy cat. He was another reason she had to get away from this guy. To go rescue her cat.

Someday someone would truly need her, and she'd probably be theirs for life. Until then, she'd just have to live with her compulsion to heal and sympathize and comfort anyone who would let her.

She used to think she could fill her need to be needed by having children of her own. But that wasn't in her future. She was infertile.

Her body moved on auto pilot. She walked closer to Romano and put a hand on his hard, broad shoulder, and she felt him tense up.

He took a deep, shuddery breath, lifted his chin, and walked into the bathroom without looking back. Lexi's hand lingered in the air for a moment.

He didn't bother to close the bathroom door behind him. But he turned toward her, every hint of human emotion once again hidden behind a granite facade. He unbuttoned his jeans.

"You might want to turn around. I'm gonna leave the door open, just in case you decide to try and run."

He lowered the zipper, hooked his thumbs in the waistband. "Or you can watch. It's all the same to me."

She managed to convince herself to turn around while he was in the process of shoving his jeans down. "I'm a doctor, Romano. No point in trying to shock me with nudity." Then she heard the water running.

Lexi chanced a quick glance over her shoulder and was rewarded with an unobstructed view of his wide back and dimpled butt cheeks. He stood in the shower curtain still open, water cascading over him, trickling down, beading up. Steam rose from his skin, and she couldn't look away.

Until he turned, and caught her looking. He seemed to pale a little bit, but before he could make some lewd comment, she turned toward the bed that was still made up. "Guess I'll try to get some sleep like you said."

He didn't reply, so she crawled under the covers, clothes and all, curled up with her back toward him, and closed her eyes.

She was, she realized, sexually attracted to Romano. A man who had basically abducted her and who was determined to destroy the life's work of her father. It was kind of sickening to admit it, but she'd never been one to indulge in denial. It was what it was. She'd just have to deal with it.

CHAPTER SIX

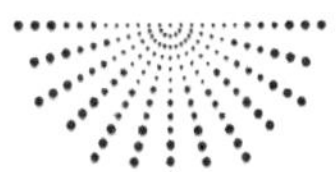

$\mathscr{H}$is bandages came loose in the shower and the wound burned like a hot brand. His injury was the least of his worries, but he'd have to take care of it all the same.

Lexi Stoltz was too smart for her own good, and too beautiful for his peace of mind. She'd seen the photograph he carried everywhere he went. When he was alone, he set it up beside his bed or sleeping bag or wherever he slept. He liked it to be the last thing he saw before sleep and the first thing he saw when he woke. So he would never forget.

Pain helped him remember. It was his pain, his private pain. Lexi had no business poking around in it. He didn't want or need to share his grief or his guilt. Especially not with her. She'd invaded his most private place when she'd reached into that pain to put her hand on his shoulder.

An offer of comfort, sure, but he didn't want her damned comfort. When she'd almost touched the photo of Wendy and the boys …

It was wrong to let anyone touch it. Especially the first woman to stir a healthy lust in him since he'd lost them. And that was wrong, too. He had to keep her away from that sacred memory, that sacred pain.

He bit his lip against the swelling in his throat and the burning in his eyes. His little boys had been his world, and Wendy had been a big part of that world.

This job, this mission was for them. He was going to avenge their deaths. And Lexi Stoltz posed a threat to that. Somehow, he knew she could prevent him from exacting vengeance and bringing down the elusive Mr. White. It didn't make sense to think that, but he trusted his gut. He couldn't let her to come between him and his goal.

He stepped out of the bathroom, wearing his shorts and nothing else. Let her be shocked. Let her throw a prissy little fit and he could despise her for being pretentious and phony.

But she didn't. She lay on the bed, curled up on one side with her back to him. Her long dark hair covered her shoulder, a few wavy tendrils reaching out over the pillow like vines in search of something to twist around. It sure as hell wasn't going to be him.

She didn't move so he figured she'd managed to fall asleep after all. Good. About time.

He fished his medical kit out of the bag and taped up his shoulder. Doing it one-handed was on the edge of impossible, but he did what he could. When she didn't offer to help, he was *sure* she was sleeping. She was too softhearted to let him struggle.

He ate. But the whole time, the image of her, lying there in the bed wearing his T-shirt now, with her hair spread around her like dark chocolate satin, haunted his mind. She hadn't eaten. She should've. She'd need her energy for the trip ahead. Either she was too fussy to settle for the MREs in his pack or she seriously wasn't hungry. Probably the latter.

He ought to wake her up and make her eat.

He didn't.

And when he'd cleaned his guns and loaded them and run out of things to do, he sat there on his own bed and looked at her.

Why did he have to end up saddled with a woman who could make a saint have impure thoughts? He far preferred the usual risks, bullets flying past his head, that sort of thing Why her?

Romano hadn't had sex with a woman since Wendy had died. And, frankly, he hadn't wanted to. That part of him had died with his family. He hadn't been aroused since the night when his life had gone up in smoke, and that was fine by him. He'd planned to just throw himself, body and soul, into the job, until one of these times, the bad guys got the best of him and put an end to this joke that passed for a life.

But work hadn't made him forget. And with a cloud of suspicion still hanging over him at the Bureau, and Stryker always watching his every move, it had become impossible to stay on the job. His former partner was convinced of his guilt in the bombing that had killed his family. Stryker had never been able to back up his suspicions, but he'd never stopped trying. Eventually, work had become impossible.

Hell, he couldn't even blame Stryker. He'd been in love with Wendy himself. But a drunken night between Romano and Wendy had led to an unplanned pregnancy and they'd decided to get married. If that hadn't happened, she probably would have ended up married to Stryker.

And maybe she'd still be alive.

Though he never said it out loud, Stryker was a constant reminder of that fact. So Romano had chosen retirement. But that hadn't worked out, either.

He'd entered stage three now, he supposed. He was living for vengeance. That was all he cared about. There was no room for sympathy or even lust.

So what was it about Lexi that had him feeling … desire?

The longer he looked at her, the more he felt it, even after almost a year without a sign of life from his libido.

Made no sense whatsoever. But he could resist temptation. If he could dodge bullets and battle terrorists, he could fight off a little coup attempt by his reborn sex drive. He wasn't going to be unfaithful to Wendy's memory. And he sure as hell wasn't going to get involved with Lexi. That would interfere with the job he had to do.

So he sat there arguing with his body until an hour before dawn. That was when she muttered something in her sleep and rolled over, bending one long leg, causing the T-shirt to bunch up around her waist. And he saw the little white cotton panties she wore, and he wanted to go over there and slide them off her.

He was undeniably turned on and disgusted with himself for it. Fresh air might help. He pulled on his jeans and T-shirt and headed out the door, paced in the parking lot, stared up at the fading night sky. But it didn't give him any answers and did little to erase this sudden hunger for a woman he barely knew.

A vehicle pulled in, grabbing his attention. The black van moved slowly through the parking lot like a shark on the hunt.

He ducked into the shadows, pressing his back to wall and moving sideways until he could see the van again. There had been two vans at Lexi's log mansion. He'd blown one to hell, but not the other. This was not some weary traveler looking for a good parking spot. It was White, or more of his henchmen.

How the hell had they followed him here? Had they seen his car? Did they know what to look for?

Didn't matter. He'd left two alive back there, two who could describe him and Lexi. He should've killed them both.

The van came to a stop out front, and someone got out and headed toward the motel office, probably to ask the clerk if anyone matching his or Lexi's description had been here.

He quickly ducked back into their room, closed the door, and went to the bed where Lexi lay sleeping, her face illuminated only by the flickering orange glow of the damaged neon vacancy sign outside. He leaned over her, touched her shoulder and whispered. "Wake up."

Her eyes opened, slow and sleepy. She stared up at him, and whispered, "But I don't even know your real name."

He swallowed hard, told himself not to dwell on the possible interpretations of that response. "We have to leave. They're here."

Her eyes rounded, and she lunged out of the bed almost knocking him over in the process. She quickly pulled on her jeans, stuffed her feet into her sneakers. "Where are they?"

"They're in the motel office now. If we get out fast, they won't hear us leave."

"How did they find us?" She ran around the room, gathering up their things, cramming them into her purse, his duffle, whatever was close. He saw the safe deposit box key tumble from her bag to the floor, then watched her snatch it up quick and shove it into her back pocket.

"Damned if I know." He scanned the room to make sure they hadn't left anything behind. As he checked the bathroom, he tried to figure it out, talking it through as he did. "I spotted the safe-deposit box receipt in your father's room. Left it there like a damned rookie."

He'd snatched up a few things, her watch and their motel-provided toothbrushes, his razor. "Once they knew where we were going and that we were in a hurry, all they had to do was take the most direct route, and start checking motels along the highway. Amateur hour. My mistake. I know better."

Her brown eyes probed his, narrowing, searching. It was as if she knew his words had some double meaning, as if she was trying, even now, to see the source of his consuming pain. The way she looked at him made him shiver, and he was damned if he knew why. He shoved everything he'd found into the duffel, slung it over his shoulder and took her arm.

He held his gun at the ready in his right hand and opened the door.

~

Lexi planted her feet when they got to the door. "I can't do this. I can't go out there." She whispered the words, but Romano pulled her through the door and outside, then quickly around the building to where he'd parked the car. She moved on legs as stiff as boards, which she figured was just as well. If her knees bent at all, they'd probably dissolve.

She tried to look around, tried to search the area for men with guns. It seemed at first that they were everywhere, but it was only that the parking lot was alive as headlights passed on the highway, making the shadows come to life. There could be twenty men in black lurking out here, and they'd be invisible.

From somewhere on the highway, music came faintly, then louder, then faded again. Motors purred and sputtered and roared. She could hear the tinny voices and canned laughter of a TV sitcom coming from one of the rooms nearby, and there was a throaty gurgle of rushing water from beneath the grate just under her feet. Nothing else. But that didn't mean they were alone.

Romano leaned close to her. "Give me that safe deposit key. But don't make it obvious."

She stared at him, but he didn't meet her eyes. His were wide, alert, moving back and forth as he scanned the parking lot.

Almost afraid to move, Lexi reached toward the back pocket of her jeans.

He turned to her all of the sudden, one arm snapping around her waist. Then he pulled her close, and his mouth covered hers. He pressed her back to the wall, nudging her mouth open, kissing her in a way she'd never been kissed before. His hand slid down over her back, and her eyes fell closed even as she realized that his remained open. And he still held a gun in his other hand.

Her legs dissolved, and she put her arms around his neck. She'd sink to the ground if she didn't. His mouth on hers was hungry as it invaded and devoured. When his hand clasped her buttocks, squeezed her there, held her hips to his, she felt her insides turn molten. She tilted her head, kissing him back as her mind spun into madness. Conscious thought fled. Feeling took over. Sensation. The blood in her veins grew lava-hot, and every nerve ending quivered. She slid her fingers into his long dark hair, even moved her hips against him. He was eliciting responses from her very soul as he kissed her. The way his hand moved, kneaded, slid …

Into her back pocket, and then out again, with the key.

He straightened away from her, the key now in his fist, his eyes just as alert and sharp as before. His breathing was normal. Hers was ragged. She pressed herself to the wall behind her to keep from falling. Her heart hammered.

He turned, scanning the lot again, unmoved by the chaos he'd just brought crashing down on her.

"Now be casual. Open the passenger door and get in."

She swallowed hard, lifting her chin. He was either a cold-hearted bastard or he was completely oblivious to the storm he'd just set loose inside her. She hoped for the latter, and walked along the passenger side of the car, toward the door. He kept pace on the driver's side.

She reached the door, put her hand on it.

"Not leaving so soon, are you, Romano? The party is only beginning."

The accent was British, and the shrill voice sent cold chills up Lexi's spine. She froze, moving only her eyes to find the source of that fingernails-on-chalkboard tone.

The man was so pale he almost glowed in the dark. He stood

right behind Romano, a gun pressed tight to the base of his neck. Romano's gaze met hers over the top of the car. There was rage in his eyes, but she sensed it wasn't directed at her. He said a single word, and it dripped with hatred.

"White."

She wondered at the accuracy of his name, then realized it was probably meant to be ironic. An albino named White. He was the essence of white. The man behind him yanked the duffel from Romano's shoulder and slung it down onto the pavement. "Your gun, my friend. Drop it."

He did. Lexi heard the clatter of metal against blacktop. She tried not to sink into a well of panic, tried telling herself it was all right. There were other guns in that duffel. Lots of other guns.

White lifted his gaze, and when it met Lexi's, she shuddered in revulsion. Cold eyes. Colorless in the darkness, only igniting with neon fire when the sign flickered and buzzed. But evil, unspeakably evil. She felt its touch when he looked at her. The neon illuminated a scar across his cheek, making it seem fresh. Goose bumps rose on her arms, and she felt a crackle of static race over her nape. He had white hair and glowing reddish eyes.

"Put those lovely arms up high, Ms. Stoltz, and come around the car to stand beside your lover, won't you?"

She opened her mouth to tell him she couldn't, but no words came out. Seemed she was scared speechless as well as motionless. Her gaze jerked back to Romano's, and he sent her a nearly imperceptible nod. Somehow, she managed to raise her hands above her head and put one foot in front of the other until she stood beside Romano, facing the car with that monster behind them.

"Turn around," the monster squeaked. His voice made her teeth hurt. Romano turned to face him. Lexi stood still, trembling until his hands touched her shoulders, turning her gently, telling her with his eyes that it would be okay.

The monster smiled. His eyes flashed red whenever the sign flickered His skin was alabaster. Shorter than Romano, though not by much, he was probably twenty pounds lighter. His long, narrow face ended in a pointed chin.

"Good to see you again, Romano. I barely trusted my instincts when my men described the agent who'd run off with Ms. Stoltz and left them bound, like calves at one of your American rodeos, on her living room floor. I almost convinced myself it was only wishful thinking. But it *is* you."

"You shouldn't be so glad about that," Romano said softly.

"I enjoy a worthy opponent. Makes the game more interesting."

"This is no game, White."

"Of course it is. Shall I tell you the rules?" He laughed softly, pressed his gun's barrel to Romano's forehead. Lexi gasped aloud.

"You have something I want," he said. "The key to Elliot Stoltz's safe deposit box. Give it to me, and I'll kill you quickly. Otherwise …" He smiled again, a slow, meaningful smile that froze Lexi's heart. "… it will be slow and extremely painful."

"What safe deposit box?" Romano's voice was low, dangerous.

The albino shook his head. "Lies will only earn your beautiful friend more pain, Romano."

"If there was a box somewhere, do you think I'd keep the key with me? You forget, White, I've dealt with you before."

"And you underestimated me then, too, as I recall. I did think it would take longer for you to take a lover, though. Is your dead wife a faded memory already?"

Lexi felt Romano stiffen beside her, and instantly thought of the woman in the photo. His wife was dead? What about the little boys?

"I'm going to kill this one, too," White went on. "Will you forget her as quickly?" His gun moved down over Romano's face, his chin, his neck, finally stopping when it pressed to the center of his chest. Then White reached out with his free hand, ran it slowly over Lexi's hair. She cringed backward, pressed her back tighter to the car, averted her face, but he still reached her. "I won't kill her fast like I did your wife, though. I'll take my time with this one. Shall I make you watch?"

Her stomach heaved and her lungs began to spasm. Lexi whirled, dropping to her knees and retching on the asphalt. She knelt there until she was spent, and when she finally stopped heaving, she knew she couldn't stand up again if her life depended on it. She collapsed against the duffel, sobs wrenching her body.

White shook his head disdainfully at her before returning his attention to Romano. "I never thought weak women were your type." He sent her a last glance, then dismissed her with a shrug. "No matter. Where is the key?"

"Not here," he said calmly, levelly.

Lexi felt her heart trip over itself. Its beat stumbled, fluttered. It was often the first sign of an episode, and she prayed it would stay in control. Her damned PSVT might get them both killed. Moving slowly, so White wouldn't know, she pawed the spilled contents of the duffel in search of her pills, as her heart switched to full blown tachycardia. Within seconds she was sucking in breaths that didn't seem enough to sustain her. She felt dizzy already.

"Where, Romano? My patience is running thin."

He only shook his head. "I can't believe you're here alone," he said. "I thought you never ventured out from under your rock without a half-dozen smaller snakes to do your dirty work."

"You bested my little snakes. And not for the first time. This is personal now, though, isn't it, Romano? Just you and I."

Lexi put her hand into the bag, knocking other items out in her frantic search for her pill bottle, still panting. She closed her fist around something cold and metallic. A gun.

She blinked in stark disbelief. She couldn't do it. Could she? Bending over herself so her long hair concealed the weapon, she took it out of the bag and turned it so the grip was in her palm and slid her finger carefully over the trigger.

"This is getting tedious," White whined in his irritating voice. "I have methods for extracting information, you know. It won't be pleasant."

Lexi didn't know if the gun was loaded. She didn't know anything about guns, except that you were supposed to pull the hammer back before firing. Only this one didn't seem to have a hammer. They had a safety switch though, didn't they? She felt around for such a switch and moved it. If she waited much longer, she'd pass out from lack of oxygen. This episode was the worst one yet. Her heart was beating so fast there was no space in between the beats. The barrel of the gun jerked in time with her racing heart as she pointed it at White.

"It's a shame. A waste of a good man. But you understand, I don't need you to lead me to the formula when I have Ms. Stoltz. And she'll be much more pleasant compan—"

She squeezed the trigger.

Romano's first thought when the shot exploded in his ears was that White had shot him. It took only an instant to realize that wasn't the case. White swore aloud, jumped backward, and swung his gun barrel toward Lexi, who still knelt on the ground.

Romano brought his fists down on White's gun hand, and the weapon dropped to the ground. White never missed a beat. He lunged away, running for all he was worth, around the building and toward the black van at the other end of the parking lot.

He wanted to go after him. To kill him. To make him pay. He

reached down to Lexi, yanking the Ruger from her cold, trembling hands.

He made the mistake of glancing at her as he did it, though, and then he paused. The red haze of his hatred faded enough so he could see her hunched on the cold pavement, holding her chest with one hand and gasping for breath. Her eyes were wide and swimming.

He heard the van door slide open. Damn. No doubt White had other weapons in there. He crouched down, spotted the pill bottle, which had rolled out of the bag, grabbed it and rapidly shoved a pill between her lips.

He stuck the gun into his jeans, bent to grip her under the arms and helped her to her feet. Their supplies were scattered and there was no time to gather them all. He grabbed the duffel as he opened the car door and slung it into the back seat. "Get in, Lexi. Quick!"

She crouched and snatched something else off the ground, then scrambled across the front seat into the passenger side.

Romano dove behind the wheel. The van was already coming toward them. He jammed the car into gear, spun the tires and they sped out of the parking lot and into traffic.

All the while, one hand was elbow deep in the console. He found what he wanted, a little cocktail for his pal, Mr. White. He anchored the bottle between his thighs, worked a lighter from his jeans pocket, flicked the flame to life and touched it to the cloth. Then he chucked the Molotov cocktail right out the back, through the missing rear windshield. It smashed onto the pavement and exploded. Cars skidded every which way, and traffic came to a complete halt.

"God, you'll kill someone!"

"Just light and noise, and it served its purpose." He nodded at the van, which was blocked by other vehicles due to the chaos he'd caused.

Then he changed lanes and passed everything ahead of him.

But even when the mess was far behind, he didn't let up on his speed. He wasn't taking any more chances with White. He couldn't afford to make another mistake.

Some miles later, finally confident of their escape, he glanced over at Lexi. She sat still, her pupils still dilated, her face flush with color. Her panting had eased, so apparently that pill had kicked in.

His photo was on her lap. Wendy and the boys, smiling and beautiful. All he had left of them, really.

A horn blew, and he jerked his attention back to the highway and swerved into his own lane, but his mind was going back over their escape. She'd grabbed something off the pavement before scrambling into the car. His photo. Why?

He looked at her again, keeping one eye on his driving this time. She was shaken up, that was for sure. "You okay?"

Her answer was a vague nod. She licked her lips. "Did … did I hurt him?"

"White?" The question surprised him.

"Did I hurt him?"

"You missed by a mile, Lexi. But you got our asses out of a tight spot, That was quick thinking. You did all right back there, for a rookie."

She closed her eyes, lowered her head. "I went into arrhythmia and almost passed out."

"You kept your head and used your wits. Not too many people I know could have done that with a killer a foot away and a heart racing out of control."

"I was looking for my pills. I found the gun by mistake."

Romano frowned, wondering why she was so determined not to take any credit. "Did you fire it by mistake, too?"

"No."

"No. You didn't save my photo by mistake either, did you?"

She said nothing for a long time.

"Thank you," he said at length.

When she finally spoke again, her voice was almost normal. "What happens now?"

He sighed. "I've been thinking on that. They know where the safe deposit box is. Saw that receipt, same as I did."

"They don't have the key, though," she said. It lacked conviction.

"Neither do we. I dropped it through the storm grate in the parking lot the second I felt his gun barrel against my neck."

"On purpose?" He nodded and she frowned even harder. "Why? Why throw it away after you went to so much trouble to take it from me?"

He looked at her quickly, trying to read the emotion in her eyes. She was still showing mostly fear, though, and it camouflaged everything else. He was impressed all over again that she'd managed to save their asses while being scared half out of her mind.

"I apologize for kissing you like that. White was watching. I could feel him, and I didn't want him to see me take the key from you. It … was the first thing that popped into my head."

Yeah, right. If he was honest, he'd admit kissing Lexi like that had popped into his head several times since they'd been thrown together. But he'd never imagined her response would be pure, mind-blowing desire. Hell, he hadn't imagined *what* her response would be, because he'd had no intention of giving in to the urge.

She'd turned to liquid fire in his arms, and he'd almost forgotten all about White and vengeance and finding the formula and saving the world. When she'd moaned in a deep, throaty voice, and opened her mouth to him, and raked his hair with her fingers …

"Don't ever do it again," she said softly, her voice somehow strong as steel despite its underlying waver.

And for some reason, that offended him. "Yeah, I could tell you really hated it."

Her eyes widened and she stared at him as if he'd turned into a spitting cobra. Hell, he kind of had. "All right, I won't lay a hand on you. Feel better?"

She looked away, staring straight ahead. "Why did you throw the key away?"

"To keep him from getting it. Not that it matters now. White knows where that box is, and hell itself won't stop him. Even if we manage to get there first, he'll be there, waiting. They'll take us out the second we step out of the building."

"Then … then it's over? We've lost?"

"Not by a long shot. I'm good at what I do. One of the best. I've just gotta figure out how I can get to the safe deposit box first, and do it without getting my head blown off. Simple."

He looked at her, and he knew the second he saw her face that there was more. Something she hadn't told him. Guilt clouded her brown eyes, and she gnawed her lower lip.

"What?"

She cleared her throat. "I can't let you risk getting shot when …"

"When …?"

"There is no safe deposit box in New York."

"What the hell do you mean? I saw the receipt."

"There was once, but I closed it after my father died."

CHAPTER SEVEN

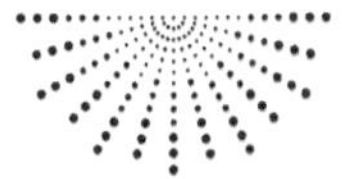

$\mathcal{R}$omano swore until he ran out of breath, then he inhaled and started over. There was an exit ramp and he took it, crossing three lanes in the process and causing other drivers to spike their brakes and shake their fists. Then he came to a stop on the shoulder in a cloud of dust. "How the hell can there not be a safe-deposit box, Lexi?"

She met his eyes, showing her backbone again. Until recently, he hadn't seen a sign of it. But she'd been playing him.

"There was one once. Just like I said, in New York. I didn't see any point in keeping it open when I had no plans to ever go back there."

The question that sprang to the tip of his tongue was why not. But he bit it back. It didn't matter what her reasons were. He didn't give a damn why a talented young doctor would want to hide herself away in the mountains alone and never emerge into the daylight again. All that mattered was finding this damned formula before White did. And then killing the bastard.

So why was it so hard to keep from asking the question?

He clamped his jaw and put the car into motion again, braking for a light at the end of the ramp, then turning right, having no idea where the hell he was going, just driving. "Go on, tell me the rest."

She looked at him with wary eyes. Half afraid of him, half hating his guts, as best he could figure. "We're on the same side, Lexi."

"No, we're not. My father is dead. I'm the only one left to protect his legacy."

Questions were burning in Romano's mind again. Questions that had nothing to do with this case. Questions about her and why she was so determined to protect a dead man who, from what he'd gleaned, hadn't been very nice to her while he'd been alive.

He forcibly resisted the urge to ask, to delve into her psyche, to search for the source of all the pain he sometimes saw in her eyes. He took the next left. "So what did you do with the contents of the box?"

"I had everything sent to my father's lawyer in Pine Lake."

"Pine Lake? That little village near your log mansion?"

She nodded. "I just wasn't up to going through any more of Father's things at the time. Jim stored everything for me, said it would be there whenever I was ready."

"You're telling me that the notes I've been searching for were up there in Pine Lake all along?"

"I'm telling you whatever my father had in that safe deposit box has been up there in Pine Lake all along, yes."

Romano rolled his eyes and sighed through clenched teeth. "And the key?"

"That was just my old PO box key. A prop."

He swore some more, pulled the car to a stop on the shoulder of the road so he could watch her face while she spoke. "So I was supposed to trot my ass all the way to New York on this wild-goose chase you set up, and then what? While I sat around trying to figure it out, you were gonna give me the slip, right? Head back up to your precious mountain retreat and grab your father's notes from that lawyer on your way?"

"And my cat."

"And then what, Lexi?"

"I don't know. All I know is my father didn't do what you think he did."

"Yeah, and I'm Santa Claus."

"I don't understand why you're so angry."

He turned toward her, gripped her shoulders in his hands, and stared right into her eyes. "Because this plan of yours could have worked! You could have pulled this off, and if you had, I'd have been completely stumped. Pine Lake would be the last place I'd have looked for you. And dammit, you'd have probably ended up dead!"

She shook her head slowly, her eyes probing his, confusion clouding their liquid brown depths.

"Dead, Lexi. Cold and stiff in the ground. No more talking or laughing or flashing those big brown eyes. Nothing. One minute you're fine, and the next … it's just all over. It's all freaking over."

His hands had tightened on her shoulders. "Over," he said, his voice lowering, growing harsher and rougher than it should. "For you, anyway. Not for me. I'd have more blood on my hands, one more innocent person dead because of me. And one more is more than I can take."

Her eyes slowly came into focus through the haze that had been clouding his vision. Her eyes, so damned intense they could see things no normal eyes could see. He knew it. He had the feeling she was reading his scarred soul just then as easily as reading a book. He gave his head a shake and he released her. But he knew it wasn't soon enough. She'd managed to shake him right out of his coldness, right out of his mannequin state, and she'd copped yet another peek at the hell that lived inside him. She'd seen way too much.

He looked away, lowering his hands from her shoulders. He steadied his breathing, but he could feel her eyes on him. And when he glanced back at her, he saw the way they darted rapidly over his face. Hesitantly, she lifted her hand, as if to press it to his cheek, but stopped in midair, maybe because of the look in his eyes.

"You're in so much pain." It wasn't a question, the way she said it. More like an observation. One that made his heart bleed. Romano didn't want her sympathy. He could handle just about anything but that.

"You're changing the subject. We were talking about you."

"No. I don't think we were."

When traffic cleared, he pulled a U-turn and headed back the way they'd come.

"She was beautiful, your wife."

He only nodded, trying to focus on driving, trying to work out his next step. Revenge. Justice. The blood and pain and death he was going to inflict on White. Those should be the only things on his mind. Ugliness, blackness, violence.

"Tell me about her," Lexi said softly, and her voice was like a whisper of music, a soothing melody that played through the noise of hate and rage in his heart. "What was her name?"

"Wendy." He said it automatically, without stopping to think about it first. Then he bit his lip, knowing he shouldn't have answered. He didn't talk about Wendy and the boys. Not to anyone.

She was silent for a moment, and Romano thought maybe she'd decided to grant him a reprieve.

"And what about your little boys?"

You don't talk about them to anyone. You don't talk about your family to anyone. You don't talk—

His thoughts were interrupted by his own raspy voice. "Justin and Jackson." Why was he talking to her? Why was he compelled to answer her gentle questions? Why didn't he just tell her to shut up and mind her own damned business?

"How old?"

"Justin was four. Jack was only two."

"No." Her hand rose to her lips and moisture filled her eyes. Then she touched him. There was no stopping her this time. Her hand covered his white-knuckled one on the steering wheel.

His foot hit the brake without his permission. The car jerked to a stop in the middle of the narrow road, and the pickup behind him blasted its horn before going around. He barely noticed. Grief blinded him, and the lump in his throat had swelled to encompass his entire chest. It was suffocating him, choking him. His hands on the wheel clenched tighter and he closed his eyes, shook his head. "I can't do this."

"Yes, you can," she whispered, just as if she knew exactly what he was talking about, even when he wasn't even sure he knew himself. "It's all right. Come here."

And he did. Damn him, he did. He turned toward her and let her pull him into her arms. She cradled his head on her shoulder, massaging the back of his neck with one hand, rubbing his back with the other. And it felt good, dammit. It felt good. So good that he put his arms around her waist and squeezed her closer. So good that he didn't pull away when she turned her head and pressed her soft lips to his cheek. He felt the moisture, the warmth between his face and hers, and he wasn't sure whose tears dampened his skin. It didn't matter. He was sinking in a stagnant sea of guilt and fury and pain. And she was suddenly there, buoyant and light, just when he'd been about to drown. Her goodness washed over him like a cleansing, fragrant wave. Somewhere inside a voice whispered, *Cling to her and save yourself, Romano. She's your only hope.*

And for one, insane moment, he did. He turned his face to her and slid his mouth over the satiny skin of her cheek and her jaw, and finally covered her lips. He felt them tremble and then part in gentle invitation. And it was an invitation he couldn't turn down. He tasted and drank from her. She was sweetness and light, innocence and fire, and he'd been without those things for so damned long they were drugging to him. Addictive. All he wanted was more of her, more of her, more of her. Because to let her go would be to return to the bleakness of reality.

It was her whispery sigh that snapped him back to sanity. And as he returned to himself, he knew what he'd done. He couldn't go on with this. It wouldn't be fair to use her that way.

Clenching his jaw, he straightened away from her. He was ashamed and embarrassed by the emotions that had swamped him. His cheeks were still wet.

So were hers. And her eyes, round and wet with glycerin tears. Her swollen lips remained parted, and he wanted them again when he looked at them. So he looked away.

He was supposed to be tough, strong. He was supposed to be in charge, protecting her from White and his thugs. Not turning to her for comfort like one of her patients. Not punishing her by letting his pain become passion and spending all of it on her. She didn't deserve that. What the hell was wrong with him? How did she manage to dig so deeply into his soul with those eyes, extracting his most painful secrets with no more than a word, a look?

"Sorry," he muttered, blinking his eyes clear. He put the car into gear, started driving again.

"There's nothing to—"

"It won't happen again."

"Maybe it should," she whispered. "Maybe you need someone right now."

"What was it, a few hours ago, you told me not to touch you again?"

She lowered her head. "I didn't know who you really were then."

"You still don't know who the hell I am. I don't discuss my family with strangers, Lexi. I am human, though, so I'd appreciate it if you'd keep your distance."

He didn't have to look at her to know his words had hurt her. He knew she winced, could see the flash of pain in her eyes without even turning his head. Too bad. She was apparently one of those females who thought she could heal the world with her soft touch and her smile and a little TLC with her incredible body. And her eyes, don't forget those. Well, she was wrong.

He was stuck with her for a few days, at most. Long enough to find the missing formula and send White to hell. That was it.

She was silent for a long time while he drove. He was, too, though his mind was working overtime. It took some effort to put his grief and the faces of his lost little boys back into the deep well of pain that used to be his heart.

It took a lot more effort to bring his thoughts back on track. A plan was what he needed. That was where his mind ought to be.

"Where are we going?" she asked him at last.

"Where do you think?"

She gave him a look that made him feel like a demon for deliberately trying to wound her. It was a defense mechanism, apparently designed specifically to keep her from getting too close to his private hell ever again. He couldn't help it. It was instinctual, and it was necessary.

"We're going back to Pine Lake," he told her. "But we have a few stops to make first."

Their half-sister Lexia Stoltz's isolated log cabin was a dream at first glance. Huge, and beautiful, set against a backdrop of pine trees and snow. But when Kira and Toni, who was officially *not* there with her, saw the blood on the snow, the dream seemed to have taken a nightmarish turn.

Kira knocked and the door swung inward slowly, creaking as if to warn them they would not like what they were about to find. She shot a look at Toni, pulled a gun, and said, "Stay here."

"Sure I will," Toni said, pulling a gun of her own. Married to a cop, with a long career dishing dirt on crime lords, she had enough experience to hold her own.

Kira supposed she ought to be grateful she'd convinced the pregnant Caitlin to stay home where it was safe. Joey had stayed home too, but was "tapping in" to the sister she'd never met. She'd promised to keep them posted. Kira wasn't expecting much. She didn't believe in psychics.

"Dr. Stoltz?" she called.

A plaintive yowl was the only reply. The place felt empty except for the fat yellow cat who came out to wind himself around their ankles. There was a giant Christmas tree without a single decoration standing in the front windows. It made her feel unspeakably sad.

Toni closed the door. Kira found a light switch and flipped it on. Then they walked in opposite directions, checking every room on the ground floor, and meeting back where they'd started.

"Anything?" Kira asked.

"Nothing. The cat followed me into the kitchen, though, so I filled his dishes with food and water. Enough to get him through a few days, at least. If we haven't found her by then, I'll come back for him."

Kira nodded, pointing with her eyes. "I'm pretty sure that's more blood, there on the stairs."

"Shit."

Together they went up the stairs to the second floor, then split up again to check every room.

From the bathroom, Tony called, "Blood and bandages in the wastebasket. Somebody dressed a wound in here."

"I've got an open bedroom window with a rope ladder hanging from it," Kira called back.

Toni joined her in the bedroom, eyeing the window. "Someone came after her, and it looks like she got away," Toni said slowly.

"Or tried to," Kira replied.

"Maybe it's time you told me why the DEA is looking for her, Kira."

"We're not, exactly. We're looking for the guy who's after her."

"For?"

"I can't tell you that."

Toni pursed her lips and tilted her head.

"Well, I'm DEA. So you can figure out where my interest lies. Although this dude has his fingers in so many pies ..." She stopped there and nodded. "His drug deals just fund his other illegal enterprises. I'm gonna have Michael check with his contacts in other agencies. CIA. FBI. See if there are any other active investigations we can coordinate with." She was texting while she was speaking.

"Michael? Your husband Michael?"

"Yeah," she said. "He's also my partner."

His sons had died, Lexi thought. Those adorable little boys in the photos who looked so much like him. They'd been taken from him without warning or reason. God, it was no wonder he was so nasty. The man was in more pain than any human being ought to bear in a lifetime. And his had come all at once.

He had let her hold him, even if it had been brief. He'd turned to her with his grief, turned to her as if for salvation. In his eyes she'd seen something she'd never seen before. A desperation, a plea he couldn't or wouldn't or didn't know how to voice. *Help me, Lexi.*

Maybe he wasn't even aware of it, but Romano was going to bleed to death from the poison arrows in his heart if he didn't pull them out and start to heal soon.

It was none of her business, though, was it? She barely knew him.

But Lexi had always been drawn to the wounded. The more serious the wound, the more she was compelled to help. It came of that need to be needed, she supposed. It was all twisted up in her psyche, knotted together with the death of her mother when she was only five years old, and with the cold, callousness of a father everyone said was a great man. Mix in the knowledge that she'd never have children of her own, and it was no wonder she was drawn to people she could nurture and heal.

Common sense ought to have some say in the matter, though, and common sense suggested she keep a safe distance from a man with cactus skin. A man who lashed out just to keep her away. A man who'd told her in no uncertain terms that he didn't want her help.

His wounds were too deep, too dangerous. The darkness inside him was devouring him, maybe already had. And if she got too close it would devour her too. She knew it would. She felt the warnings prickling up and down her spine and dancing over her skin. *Stay away*, they whispered. *Stay away.*

If she had any sense at all, she'd heed those warnings.

She would try, she vowed in silence. She would try to keep a cool distance. She'd stop asking about his beautiful, lost family. She'd stop caring about his pain. He was nothing to her; why should she care? She'd force herself not to reach out to him again. She could do that. It wasn't such an impossible task.

They rode in silence through the small town they'd discovered nearby, pulling in at a used car dealership where Romano went inside.

Alone in the car, Lexi couldn't help wondering if he'd been a different man before his wife and sons had died. She tried to picture him happy, content, affectionate. But it was a terrible stretch of the imagination.

"Mrs. Jones?"

There was a tap on her window and Lexi jumped, then turned to see the round, friendly face of a salesman staring in at her. She put the window down.

"Mrs. Jones, come take a look. We can't have your husband making a purchase this important without your input now, can we?"

Frowning, she opened the door and got out, allowing the salesman to lead her around the lot to where Romano was just stepping out of a motor home the size of a tank. He met her confused gaze and smiled ... *actually smiled* at her. The perfect image of the devoted husband. He crossed to where she stood, draped an arm around her shoulders.

"Well, honey, what do you think?" He waved his free hand toward the house on wheels.

His arm felt warm and heavy on her shoulders. She resisted the urge to lean into his embrace, to tilt her head sideways until it rested on his shoulder, to slide her own arm around his waist and give it a squeeze and tell him that he was going to be all right.

The man did not want to be comforted, she reminded herself.

"I ... uh ... I'm not sure *what* to think."

"It has everything. Perfect for our trip. Go on inside, take a look."

She blinked at him. He'd converted himself into the image of the American sightseer, evoking images of campfires and hot dogs.

Without a word she stepped into the camper, but she wasn't really looking at it. She just walked around, pretending to check it out, while he chatted outside with the salesman.

When he poked his head inside, he was back to his former, cold demeanor. "Get our stuff out of the car and stash it in here while I finish up the paperwork."

He said it as if he expected her immediate compliance. So she said, "No."

"What do you mean, 'no'?"

His eyes were sapphire chips. His words fell like icy rain, chilling her right to the bone. "I mean, no. You can't just give orders and expect me to carry them out. I don't work for you."

He sighed, lowered his head and pulled the camper door shut. "What do you want, Lexi?"

"I want to know the plan. I want to know why we're buying a used RV and where we're taking it. And how the hell you explained the busted-out rear window in the Porsche, or didn't he even ask about that?"

He took a slow breath and she got the feeling he was struggling for patience. "He did ask."

"And?"

"And it was a freak accident. Chunk of ice slid off a roof and right through the window."

"Why are we changing vehicles?" she asked.

"Because White's seen the car."

"But why a camper? Why not a pickup truck or a mini-van or a compact? Why this huge RV?"

"Why all the questions?" he countered. "Look, I do this kind of thing for a living. I know my job, okay?"

He'd looked into her eyes as he'd snapped his reply, but when she flinched, he looked away. She thought she glimpsed guilt, just for a second. Maybe he didn't like hurting her.

"The last thing White would find suspicious is a vehicle like this," he said, and his tone was kinder. "And having a place to sleep might come in handy. No more ambushes in motel parking lots. We can't exactly take up residence at your house in the woods again, Lexi. Hell, White probably left men posted there in case we come back."

"I don't think he'd have any reason to do that." She thinned her lips, tilted her head, still not looking at him. "So that's the plan, we're heading back to Pine Lake?"

"Yeah, to get the contents of your father's safe deposit box from his lawyer."

"And then?"

He shook his head. "I don't know. That's all I've got. I guess it depends on what we find." He looked at her again. "Okay?"

"Yeah. Okay."

CHAPTER EIGHT

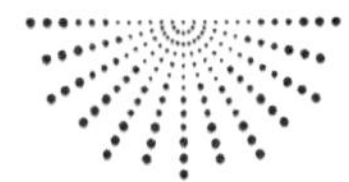

"**Y**ou were right about Lexi Stoltz being in trouble," Kira said to Joey. They'd returned to Toni and Nick's gorgeous Victorian, which had become their base of operations, mainly because it had room for all of them and was closest to where all the action seemed to be happening. "We found blood and bullet casings in the snow outside, more blood in the house—"

"She's okay though," Joey said with a reassuring look Cait's way. "She got out. She had to climb … a rope or something."

"Rope ladder," Toni confirmed. "It was still hanging from the bedroom window."

Kira gaped from Joey to Toni and back again.

"What?" Joey asked "I *told* you—"

"Yeah, you told me, but I didn't *believe* it." She frowned at the half-sister with the wavy hair in every shade of blonde from ash to caramel. "You really *do* have it, don't you?"

"Yeah. I really do. Sometimes I wish I didn't. But right now it's good. Right now it's telling me our sister Lexia is okay. Scared. On the run, but okay." She frowned and added, "And it's Lexi. She hates being called Lexia."

"I'll make a note."

"What are we going to do now, though?" Cait asked. "She's running scared and bad guys are chasing her, and she probably doesn't even know we're out here, waiting to help. She might not even know we exist. How can we find her?"

Kira sighed, lowering her head. "My husband's FBI contact says the guy we think is after her was seen at a motel off 81, near where that crazy accident happened in the wee hours this morning."

"The one where the guy was throwing homemade bombs at other cars?" Cait asked, a catch in her voice.

"Molotov," Joey muttered.

Kira nodded. "Right. Not bombs, really. Nothing that was going to do anyone any harm. Most of law enforcement is calling it a prank. One little Molotov cocktail, lots of flash, not much else."

"It was a diversion. So they could get away." Joey said it as if it was a proven fact.

Kira was about finished doubting her sister's abilities. She said, "You think Lexi threw that cocktail, Joey?"

"Not her. The sexy as sin guy who's with her."

Caitlin and Toni exchanged a raised-eyebrow look. Kira fired off a text to Michael. "This is good, if you're right," she said while tapping her phone.

"Why?" Joey asked.

Kira held up a hand as Michael's reply popped onto her phone's screen, then read it aloud, but slowly, so she could stop if she came to anything classified. "They pulled a print off a piece of the bottle bomb. It belonged to a former FBI explosives expert name of Connor Romano. Nickname ..." She looked at Joey. "Molotov."

"Former FBI? Why'd he leave?" Toni asked.

Kira texted, then waited, then swore under her breath. "His wife and two kids were murdered, possibly by the same guy who's after Lexi. It was a bomb. And there are some in the Bureau who think he was involved."

"Our sister's with a man capable of blowing up his own family?" Caitlin asked a little breathlessly. "God, why are these animals after her, and how are we going to find her?"

The clouds overhead were ominous as Lexi and Romano got out of the RV in the parking lot of a diner just off the highway. Romano was watchful, suspicious of every stranger who so much as glanced in their direction. Lexi looked around in a much different way as they headed for the diner, then she paused and pointed. "Look, there's a Walmart across the street. Maybe we ought to pick up some supplies before we leave."

"Good idea."

In the diner, Romano was uneasy. Too many eyes on them, eyes that could describe them later, should White stop by asking questions. But he figured the chances of the bastard checking every diner in every town were slim. And since he'd expect them to continue south, they were even slimmer.

No one in the place seemed to be paying undue attention to them. He breathed a little easier and headed up to the counter. Lexi was already there, ordering a club sandwich and a soda to go in that deep, smoky voice that made a person really listen when she spoke. He stepped up beside her.

"You two together?"

He blinked at the waitress's question. Lexi said, "Yeah," and she looked

up at him.

He had trouble pulling free of her eyes, but managed to do it, and gave the waitress a curt nod. "Just double her order."

Lexi was still looking at him. He felt the touch of her eyes as the waitress punched keys on an old-fashioned cash register that chucked and pinged. He took the wallet from his pocket, handed over cash and waited for the change. Why did she find it necessary to *look* at him like that? It always felt like she was probing his damn soul.

There was a country song coming from a radio somewhere. Another waitress was busy tacking strands of green garland to the edges of the counter, reminding him of the approaching holiday season. Someone had sprayed the place with a pine-scented air freshener.

A memory slipped into his mind. He heard Justin's laughter and Jack's high pitched squeals of delight, and the crinkling and tearing of gift wrap.

The flashback was brief, but vivid, real. And it took him by surprise, because he'd denied himself any real memories for a year and a half. He'd never been able to think back to happy times, only to that night, that explosion that had ended them forever.

The bell over the entrance jangled and he glanced behind him, watching his back as he always did. And then he felt a hot blade slip right into his chest and twist slowly, tearing his insides to shreds.

The little boy who'd come in was no more than five. All dark curls, baby blue eyes and dimples as he grinned up at his father, his tiny hand enfolded in a much bigger one. They moved inside, talking and laughing, choosing a table.

Romano felt the black emptiness in his soul reaching up to claim him. It drew him into the depths of despair, back into his endless grief. He closed his eyes to blot out the image of the happy pair.

They should've been outside playing. Dammit, why the hell hadn't the boys been outside? They never came in until Wendy called them for dinner. Never. The fenced in back yard was their favorite place in the known universe. The fort he'd built them, in that young hard maple tree. The jungle gym. The swings.

He felt a warm, firm hand on his shoulder and swung his head around. Lexi's eyes were wider and browner than ever, and they were damp as they met his. He hated that his pain was so clear to her. It was coming to the surface more than it had in months and he didn't know why.

Something about her. Something about Lexi.

He gave his head a slight shake. "I'm gonna hit that store across the street for supplies like you suggested, if you're okay here." His voice sounded like he'd gargled with gravel.

"Yeah, I'm fine."

He nodded, turned, and walked out of the diner. The door swung closed on the little boy's laughter and Romano blinked in the crisp December air, wishing it was colder, wishing it could slap his face and snap him out of this grief. But it wasn't and it didn't. Nothing ever had. Maybe nothing ever would.

Lexi stared after him. Part of her wanted to go to him, try to help him through the haze of pain he was obviously battling. But another part knew he wanted to be left alone.

"Miss?"

She turned back to the counter to see the woman on the other side holding out a handful of change. Lexi took it. "Is there a restroom I can use while I'm waiting for the sandwiches?"

The woman nodded, pointing toward the back of the building. Lexi tried to put Romano's heartache out of her mind as she walked into the ladies' room. She took her time, washed her face, combed her hair, dug through her purse and applied a little bit of makeup she'd found in there. Eventually, she stopped and just stared at her reflection in the mirror, telling herself she was not Romano's only hope of salvation. She wasn't. He didn't want her to be, and more importantly, she didn't want to be.

Some twenty minutes later, when she pushed the door open to head back out, she glanced up to see a man dressed all in black leaning on the counter where she'd been standing. And for just a second, she stiffened. It was that color that did it. Everything black, right to the knit cap on his head. He had everything the thugs at her house had, except the mask and guns.

She started to think she had an overactive imagination. And then she saw the waitress looking at the guy's cell phone, nodding as her lips formed the word "restroom" and her head tilted toward where Lexi stood.

As if in slow motion, the man's head started to turn toward her. She ducked back inside before he could see her, closed the door and turned its lock.

Her heart did a little jumpity-jump in her chest. "Not now," she whispered. "Not now, my pills are in the RV." She leaned over the sink, wet a paper towel with cold water and slapped it onto the back of her neck. What should she do?

She scanned the restroom. There was one squat window on the back wall, too high to reach from the floor. Lexi looked around for something to stand on, and settled on the trash can. It only took a second to remove the rounded top and flip the can upside down. She silently apologized for the mess as she climbed up. The window locked from the inside, and she turned the clasp to the unlocked position, mentally crossed her fingers and shoved it upward. It opened easily, and she thanked her lucky star and climbed up on the ledge, peering outside first. She saw no one, but there was no way to be sure. Well, she couldn't just sit there waiting for the jerk to get sick of being patient and come in after her.

She slipped over the edge, turned and lowered herself until she dangled a few feet above the ground, then let go and landed with an ungraceful tumble. She looked around, hoping she hadn't been seen as she got to her feet and brushed the dust from her jeans. Then she hurried back to where the RV was parked out front, keeping the oversized vehicle between her and the diner.

Romano was already inside and Lexi thought she'd never been so glad to see anyone in her entire life. He stood in the tiny kitchen area, unloading a bag of groceries into the cupboards. Or pretending to. Actually, he was waiting. For her, she realized. He was probably expecting her to try to comfort him again, the way she'd done before. And dreading it.

She took a couple of steadying breaths, went right to the front, sat down in the driver's seat and started the motor. Then she put the thing in gear and pulled slowly out of the parking lot.

A second later, Romano was standing behind her, one hand on her shoulder, but only to steady himself, she was sure. "What's going on?"

"One of them … back there, in the diner." She bit her lip. Her words were coming out in bits and pieces, and her heart was starting to beat too fast again.

"Easy," he said, and his hand squeezed her shoulder. She closed her eyes because it felt so good. "Drive nice and slow, Lexi. Take your time. No one's gonna look twice at a camper, unless it's careening through town, taking curves on two wheels."

She eased up on the accelerator, nodding, willing her heart to slow down and not launch into a full-blown episode. Safe now, she kept telling herself. She was safe now.

"You need this?" Romano held her prescription bottle in one hand. She hadn't even seen him reach for it.

"I don't think so."

He returned it to the glove compartment. "Tell me what happened."

"I went to the restroom. When I started to come out there was a man at the counter, dressed all in black. He was showing his phone to the waitress, and the waitress pointed toward the restroom. I was the only one in there."

"And?"

"I ducked back inside before he saw me, locked the door and climbed out the window." She looked up at him to gauge his reaction to that, and was surprised to see him smile a little. "What?"

"The idiot's probably still sitting there waiting for you to come out."

"Do you think it was—"

"I have little doubt it was one of White's henchmen. Just as we pulled out, I spotted a black van parked nearby. How the hell they found us, I don't know. Maybe they didn't. Maybe they're just looking, checking motels and diners up and down 81."

"I was sure I'd overreacted."

"You didn't overreact. You did exactly what I would've done. Never hesitate to follow your instincts."

"I didn't get our sandwiches."

"We'll get some more sandwiches. Actually, I grabbed everything we need to make sandwiches. Some clothes too."

She bit her lower lip, turned to look at him again. "I'm really scared."

"I shouldn't have left you alone in there."

"It's all right," she said quickly.

"It's not all right." He drew a breath, let it out slowly and finally moved up to sit opposite her in the passenger seat. "It's been eighteen months," he said softly.

Lexi almost gasped in surprise. Was he actually going to tell her about his family?

"I worked for the FBI, and I thwarted one of White's bigger projects. He'd been contracted to blow up a government building in Albany. I pulled his trigger early, blew up his mercenaries instead. In return, he blew up my house. My family."

"Oh my God. I'm so sorry."

"I ought to be handling things better by now."

"It … can't be easy. And eighteen months, that's barely any time at all."

He was staring straight ahead, deep in thought. Lexi had to make an effort to keep her eyes on the road. "After it happened, I resigned. I couldn't focus on the job anymore. And there are some people who suspect I was involved."

"How could anyone think that? It's insane. I barely know you, and I wouldn't believe that for a minute."

He looked at her for an extended beat, taking that in, it seemed.

"But you came back out of retirement," she prompted when he couldn't seem to find his voice again.

"Not exactly. I have friends still on the job. My former boss, Darren, is one of the closest. He let me know White was after your father's formula. Asked me to freelance the case. No one's gone up against White more times than I have. I agreed. I thought I could handle it. But I'm not doing too great so far, am I?" He gave a sad smile. "It's bringing everything back."

"It's forcing you to grieve. I don't imagine you have yet. I think you probably pushed your grief down, buried it, tried to just … keep going."

"It was working fine, up 'til now."

"You only think it was working fine. It wasn't. You've been dead inside. Dead people can't feel. But you're coming back to life, and that means you have to feel again. That's what the living do, Romano. We feel. We laugh and we cry, we celebrate and we grieve, we fight and we love. We *feel*."

He lowered his eyes, then said, "Turn left at this light. We need to get back on the highway up ahead."

She did as he said, waiting for him to continue, but her own mind was filling with new thoughts, new fears. One, in particular, that wrapped an icy hand around her heart and chilled it through and through. "Romano?"

"Yeah?"

"You said you only agreed to take this case when you realized White was involved. Will you tell me why?"

He laughed, but it wasn't really a laugh. More like a short burst of air being forced from his lungs. "He murdered my family, Lexi. Why do you think?"

CHAPTER NINE

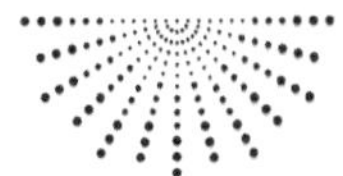

They passed the Welcome to Pine Lake sign just after nightfall. If Lexi hadn't known the place so well, she might have let Romano drive right through. Pine Lake was just a stretch of road with a few more houses than other places along the same route. The general store was the focal point. It was a repurposed airplane hangar and carried everything from food to auto parts. An ancient red gas pump tilted drunkenly to one side out front.

Romano pulled the RV off the narrow road but left it running.

"So now what?" Lexi was uneasy, and she knew he could hear that in her voice, but she'd never been very good at disguising her feelings. She just wasn't sure why she felt as much dread as she did.

"Now, we go talk to your lawyer friend and get our hands on whatever your father was keeping in his safe deposit box."

"There's not going to be anything there," she whispered. But she wasn't as sure of that as she had been at the beginning of all this. There had to be some reason everyone from international terrorists to secret agents thought otherwise. Still, she wanted to believe it was all a mistake.

She didn't want to look at Romano. Didn't want him to see the doubt that must show in her eyes. So she stared up at the gray clouds skittering over the moon like ghosts, a shade paler than the dark sky. "It's going to snow."

"Probably."

"We ought to go up to the house."

"No."

"If it snows, we might not be able to. It can come down heavy."

"Snow melts, Lexi."

She bit her lip to keep from arguing. Jax hadn't been fed today. He'd be climbing the walls by now, if those thugs they'd left at her house hadn't done something to him.

She knew she was worrying about her pet partly because it kept her from thinking about what had been in that safe-deposit box, or why her father had kept it even after breaking every other tie he'd had to his former life.

"Where does the lawyer live?"

Romano had a one-track mind.

"Just keep driving. It's a big house at the north edge of town, on the right. I'll tell you when we get there." Why was she having all these doubts now? Her father was innocent. She knew that. There'd be nothing but proof of that at Jim's office, which was no more than a converted spare room in his house's basement.

Romano put the rig back in gear and pulled onto the road again. In a few minutes, they were turning into the driveway of James McManus, attorney-at-law. A light snow had begun falling, illuminated by their headlights.

Romano walked beside her to the front door. She didn't think he could tell how terrified she was of what they would find. If her father had been working on something awful, that would explain his actions at the end. She hated that it all added up. Then again, senility or stroke also made sense, she assured herself.

She didn't realize she'd frozen on the top step until Romano's arm slid around her shoulders, squeezed just a little. "It isn't gonna matter what's there, Lexi. It can't hurt your father now."

She lifted her chin, turning to look him in the eye. "It can hurt me, though."

"You can handle it." His hand cupped her chin, and his eyes searched hers as if he truly cared what she was feeling. "You're tougher than you think, Lexi Stoltz. You've proven that. A couple of times."

"Yeah? If I'm so tough, why am I shaking right now?" She gazed into his eyes, and noticed that they were staring at her lips, like he wanted to kiss her again. And she wanted it, too.

A dog started barking from the next place over. The noise drew her gaze, and she saw curtains parting, then a face peering out at them. The neighbor's dog kept up his barking, which in turn made her wonder where the McManus's beagle was, and why *he* wasn't barking. She turned, staring first at the door, and then at the rest of the house, noticing for the first time the darkened windows and the way the cold wind riffled the pages of three newspapers lying on the porch.

"I don't think anyone's here."

He followed her gaze, then left her standing there while he ran down the steps and over to the garage to peer through the glass. "No car inside. *Dammit.*"

Lexi poked the doorbell with her forefinger, let up and poked again. But even when she gave up and started knocking instead, there was no response.

"Three newspapers," Romano muttered, coming back to the porch. "Looks like they might be gone for a while."

"They never go away for very long."

"It's the holiday season, though."

"That's right, it is. I forgot about that." Romano frowned at her, and she shrugged. "It's been a while since I've celebrated the holidays."

His lips thinned. He was going to say something nasty about her father, she thought, but he bit it back. Instead, he just said, "I've skipped them lately, too."

That admission made Lexi's eyes sting. "We can check down at the store. Someone will know when they're due back."

"Or we can break in and get what we need tonight."

"No!" She was so shocked at his suggestion that her jaw fell and her eyes widened. "We can't go around breaking into people's homes."

He shrugged. "Maybe *you* can't—"

"Romano, please. These people are friends of mine." She glanced again at the house next door, pointed at the face still peeking through the window. "We can't do it right now, anyway. We'd be seen. Let's at least wait until later, when the neighbors are in bed."

He sighed—in disgust at her reluctance, she was sure—but finally nodded. "Okay, all right, but it has to be tonight. We don't have time for finesse, Lexi."

"I know."

Relieved, she turned and headed back to the RV. He followed and soon they were driving again, through snow that fell thicker with every passing second. Romano was looking for a hidden spot to park for the night, and Lexi was worrying about her cat. So she directed him to an old fire trail cut out of the forest. He followed her directions but looked less happy about it the farther they drove. The snowfall had already coated the narrow dirt trail, but not enough to make driving hazardous. Not yet, anyway.

"This seems like it's taking us awfully close to your house, Lexi. Are you playing games with me?"

"No games," she told him as he chose a spot off the fire trail in a little copse of pines, and drove carefully onto it. "The house *is* nearby. If you follow the fire trail for a half mile, and then veer off to the right and cut through the pines, you'll end up in my father's *precious* backyard vegetable garden."

Romano shut the motor off, then the lights. "You say that as if you're not overly fond of vegetables."

"He spent more time digging in that dirt than he did with me," she blurted before thinking better of it.

"But he was a saint, all the same, right?"

She lowered her head. "I loved him."

"But he didn't love you back, did he, Lexi?"

A single tear fell. It dropped from her cheek to splash onto the back of Romano's hand, just as he reached out to cup her face. His thumb ran over her cheekbone, and he lifted her head to look into her eyes.

"You should have been disappointed in him, not the other way around. You need to open your eyes and see that one of these days. He didn't deserve a daughter like you."

"I thought I asked you not to talk about my father."

"I was talking about you."

She shook her head slowly, taking her gaze from his. "I want to go home," she whispered. "I want to go up to the house." And for the first time, she realized why. It wasn't Jax. It was that the place had become a haven in her mind. She'd run away from her entire life. Her father's failing health had just been an excuse. She'd been hiding there, had stayed even after his death. And she wanted to hide there again.

"We can't go back, not just yet. Try to be patient, okay?"

She'd try. But, God, she craved space. Room, lots of it, between Romano and her. It was killing her to be this close to him and pretend nothing had happened between them. Which was exactly what he expected, even silently demanded, that she do. She needed space, time alone, to come to grips with the very real possibility that her loyalty to her father had been sorely misplaced. She'd always known he wasn't a very *nice* person. Not a very honorable person. He'd certainly never been a very *kind* person.

Your father is a great man.

That oft-repeated refrain played through her brain like a skipping vinyl record. So many people had said it to her, beginning with her mother.

But what if he hadn't been so great after all? And what if she'd only loved him so, so much because she'd had no one else to love?

"Okay?" Romano repeated.

"Yeah. Okay." She turned in the seat, looking back into the living quarters of the RV, squinting in the darkness. "So what do we do for light and heat?"

"Propane. The dealer threw in a full tank. I just have to go outside and hook it up." He tilted his head. "Loan me my jacket and I'll do it right now."

She'd been wearing his jacket for lack of anything else. Chivalrous of him, and unexpected, but nice. She liked wearing his coat. It smelled like him, and it was almost as warm as being held in his arms.

She shrugged out of the coat and handed it to him. Romano put it on and went into the back, bending to one of the cupboards and emerging with a flashlight and an oversized pipe wrench.

"Where did you get that?"

"Pipe wrench came with the camper. I picked the flashlight up at the store while you were playing hide-and-seek with the goon in the diner. I grabbed some extra clothes, too. They're in the drawer under the bunk. Sweatshirts, heavy socks, an extra pair of jeans for each of us."

"That's good. Tell me there's a three-pound flannel nightgown in there, too."

"What do I look like, an idiot?" He tugged up the zipper of his jacket, flipped up the collar and opened the door while Lexi was still feeling the rush of heat in her cheeks.

He paused in the doorway, swearing softly.

"What's wrong?" she asked him.

"It's really coming down out there. The road must be damned near impassable by now."

"Oh." She'd figured it would be. She'd seen those low hanging clouds too often not to know when a storm was about to cut loose.

"No way in hell we'll get back to the lawyer's house tonight."

She'd been counting on it. "It's just as well," she said. "Maybe by the time the roads are cleared they'll be back."

"And maybe you planned it that way."

She shrugged. "Maybe I did."

He shook his head. "Tomorrow, Lexi. The second the roads are cleared. And I don't care if I have to break in with the whole damn town watching." With that he walked out the door, closing it behind him.

So this was it, at least for tonight. And they were together in even closer quarters than they'd been in the motel. How was she ever going to sleep? Even in bunk beds, she'd be too close to him. Way too close.

Romano came back inside ten minutes later and stood in the doorway brushing snow from his shoulders. She went to help, dusting the white stuff from his jacket. She reached for his dark hair, ruffling it with her fingers to shake the snow away. And then she stopped. His hair was soft and damp, and her fingers were buried in it. She stood very close to him, too close, maybe, and when she looked up, he was staring right down into her eyes.

He laid his hands gently over hers, still buried in his hair, and he lifted them away. Lexi blinked, turning abruptly. "Do we have matches?"

"Top drawer," he said, and she thought his voice was the slightest bit gruff.

Of course it was, he'd just been out in the cold.

She found the matches. "Better get the pilots lit. Shine the light, will you?"

He did, and Lexi lit the little gas lamps and then turned the knobs. In seconds the lamps glowed, washing the camper in warm light. It did erotic things to a man's skin, that amber glow. It did even more disturbing things to his eyes. She lit the pilot on the small two-burner range next. The camper was too old a model to have electric pilot ignition. She handed the matches to Romano. "You can do the heat. I haven't got a clue."

He nodded, took the matches from her and fiddled around in the little closet next to the cubby-sized bathroom. The place was toasty a few minutes after he emerged.

Romano shrugged off his coat and sat down at the table. So now what, Lexi wondered. She poked around in the cupboards to see what he'd bought to eat, finally settling on a can of beef stew and some instant hot cocoa. She located a can opener, some bottled water, and a pair of small pots.

"You don't have to go back there with me tomorrow," she said at last, unsure whether she'd be treading on forbidden ground to broach the subject that had been on her mind since they'd left Jim's house. I'll go alone, get the papers and bring them back here."

"Sure you will. Or maybe you'll decide to take off for parts unknown with them."

She sank into the seat across from him. "I won't do that."

"You'd do just about anything to protect your father's name, Lexi."

"Not his name, his legacy. His team at the university are working on major things. My father's reputation is what keeps them funded. There's more at stake here than just his name."

She lowered her eyes and added, "And if I tell you I won't do something, then I won't."

"Even if those papers prove your old man did exactly what I told you he did?"

She held his gaze and nodded. "Yes, even then." She wanted to add that she knew that wasn't going to be the case, but her doubts were too strong, and growing all the time. "I'll swear on his memory, if it'll make you feel better."

He searched her face for a long moment, finally nodding. "I almost believe you would. But I'm going with you, anyway."

"You … you might not want to."

He sighed heavily and let his chin fall to his chest. "I saw the bicycles in the garage. I know they have kids."

She got up, turning to the range to stir the stew, and she wondered if talking about this would hurt him more or help him. "Their grandchildren stay with them quite often. Especially during the holidays. I hadn't thought about it before, but chances are if they do get back tomorrow, they'll have the kids with them. You don't have to put yourself through that."

"Don't."

"I saw your face at that diner. I saw what looking at that little boy did to you. I'd have to be blind not to see it."

"Don't," he repeated.

"Going there tomorrow will only hurt you more." She was thinking of more than just the children. She was thinking of the things scattered all over the place that would remind Romano of his lost little ones. Toys and books and games and small clothes. There would be evidence of the children everywhere.

He lifted his chin, met her eyes without blinking. "Nothing could hurt me *more*, Lexi. Pain is something I've learned to live with."

"But—"

"And it's my pain, not yours. It has nothing to do with you, do you understand that?"

She blinked at him, wanting with everything in her to reach out and touch him, take him in her arms and make it all right for him.

"I want you to leave it alone." He got up, reaching past her to snap the burner off. "You're burning the stew."

"Romano ..."

He froze her with a single glance. "Just leave it alone, Lexi. Please."

She swallowed hard, bit back the flood of words that wanted to escape. Words of comfort that would do little good anyway. She clenched her jaw, closed her eyes. "I don't suppose you thought to buy plastic flatware, did you?"

When she opened her eyes again she saw his shoulders sag in relief, heard the breath escape him in a long sigh. "Yeah. I hate plasticware." He reached past her again, scraping open another drawer to reveal a handful of stainless set of silverware. "I grabbed a couple of plates and coffee mugs too. No bowls though. Guess we make do."

"Guess so."

Lexi left off the topic of his sons, and Romano was grateful, because it was harder with her. He still hadn't figured out why that was, but when Lexi started poking at his wounds, he couldn't stop himself from cooperating, answering her questions, opening up to her and letting her in. He didn't like that power she seemed to have over him. To make him talk about it, to invade his darkness with her light.

He didn't discuss his family with anyone. They were sacred, and that was that.

He looked at Lexi whenever she wasn't looking at him— which wasn't often—and tried to figure out what it was about her that made him forget his own rules. But there were no answers in her soft brown eyes, or in the way she managed to shovel beef stew into her mouth like a half-starved person, while still looking graceful and feminine. Didn't make a damn bit of sense.

And then her eyes caught his in the act of staring, but they were wide, startled. She swallowed hard and said, "Did you hear that?"

"Hear what?"

"Shh!" She held up a hand, tilted her head to one side.

Romano listened, and in a second he heard it, too. The distinct sound of footfalls in the wet snow. His muscles tensed, and before he was aware of moving, his gun was in his hand. Lexi moved only enough to crank a window very slightly open.

The sounds came more clearly then. Closer. A few steps, then silence, then a few more steps. Someone was creeping up on them.

Romano looked into her eyes. Big mistake. She was terrified, and it made a lump come into his throat. Made his stomach clench. "Don't be scared, Lexi, you'll get your heart going again." His thoughts should have been on other things. Like surviving a sneak attack, not comforting a scared woman. "I'm not gonna let anyone hurt you. Promise."

Stupid, making promises he knew damned well he might not be able to keep. And she wasn't much better, because she actually looked as if those words eased her mind. As if she believed him, trusted him to protect her.

Sure, just like Wendy and my sons did once.

He closed his eyes to block out thoughts like that. This was no place for them. Slowly he got up, reaching to douse the lights so he wouldn't be perfectly silhouetted when they opened the door. "Put on my jacket, just in case you have to run."

He heard the denim brushing over her as she complied. Then she was beside him, near the door. "I'll step out first," he told her. "You come out behind me, but as soon as your feet hit the ground, slip around behind the camper. I'm pretty sure there's only one of them. If anything happens to me, run down toward town. Okay?"

"No."

He froze with his hand on the doorknob, turned to study the shape of her face in the shadows.

"I'm not going anywhere if something happens to you. You might … need me."

Those two words, *need me,* came out on a trembling breath. Unsteady. As if they were inordinately important.

Oh, great, something more about her for his mind to insist on analyzing while he knew he ought to be planning this mission. Just what he needed.

"If I tell you to run, you'd damn well better run," he told her. He thought she nodded, but wasn't sure. The footfalls drew nearer, got louder.

Romano flung the camper door open and lunged through it, landing in the deep snow with his gun leveled at where the sounds had come from. And at that moment, the storm clouds skittered away from the full moon, giving him a clear glimpse of the intruder as it leapt away. A white-tailed deer with antlers that resembled a coat rack.

He was still trying to unclench his muscles when Lexi's laughter came through the crisp cold air like the clearest bell ringing from the steeple of a country church.

He turned, battling a sheepish grin of his own that refused to be contained. "Oh, so you think that's funny?"

She stood in front of the camper, nodding hard. "Of course not," she managed to say. "I'm just overcome with gratitude that you saved me from that killer buck."

Romano stuffed the gun into the waistband of his jeans to free his hands. Then he scooped up a snowball and let her have it. Splat! Dead center of her forehead.

Her laughter came to an abrupt stop about the time his began in earnest. "Why you …"

She squatted to arm herself for retaliation, but he ran before she could launch the first volley. He got pegged twice in the back as he ducked behind the camper. Then he jumped out again and got her in the chest.

She fired three at him, one after the other, and he took one in the face before he had a chance to weave out of the line of fire.

Time to change tactics. When Justin used to ambush him with snowballs this little trick had never failed. He let her hit him with one, then fell down onto his back, and lay very still, not moving.

Sure enough, she tiptoed closer.

"Romano?"

And still closer.

"Come on, Romano, I didn't hurt you, did I?"

And closer yet. She crouched down, her hands moving to touch his face, and he sprang the trap. Grabbed her shoulders and flipped her onto her back in the snow while she yelped in surprise. He straddled her to hold her still and drizzled a little white stuff onto her face while she wriggled beneath him, his head full of memories. In his mind he saw Justin's smile, heard the music of his laughter.

And then he stopped and sat very still. My God, he'd remembered. He'd done it without a flash of blinding pain. He'd been laughing. Laughing out loud.

He stared down at the woman beneath him. Her cheeks cherry red in the moonlight and falling snow, her eyes sparkling, her hair spread over the snow, damp with it.

She smiled softly. "All right, I surrender. You win. You're a superior warrior, I admit it."

He got off her, took her hands and helped her to her feet. He didn't know what to say, what to think. Part of him knew he ought to feel bad for remembering without pain. How could he? How could he play and laugh when his little boys were dead because of him?

But there was another part, a long-starved, craving part that sighed in relief. A lifeless, barren place in his soul absorbed what had just happened the way the desert absorbs the rain. And it felt like a single blade of new grass was struggling to break through.

That sensation was life, he thought. But he didn't deserve life. So he ignored it.

"I didn't know you had a playful bone in your body, Romano," she said, brushing snow away from her clothes, then starting on his.

"I …" He couldn't answer her. He was still too overwhelmed.

"I'm glad you do," she said. "I never had anyone to be playful with. I didn't even know I had it in me."

He forced himself to take his eyes off her. She looked like a kid, her hair tousled and snowy, her face glowing, her eyes sparkling.

Damn, damn, damn, he didn't like what he was feeling.

"Come on, let's go inside," she said.

He followed her, reminding himself over and over why he was there. He had to kill White. He had to avenge his family. He didn't deserve happiness, because it was his fault they were dead, and even killing that murderer wasn't going to change that. Nothing would. His family was dead and Romano was alive. That was so wrong, so very wrong that the gods must have gone off duty on that blackest of days. Fate must have taken a vacation, because it just wasn't the natural order of things. It was out of whack. The whole freaking universe was screwed up.

And he wasn't going to forget that it should have been him blown into so many bits there hadn't been enough left to bury. Those markers, standing over empty graves, should have his name cut into their stone faces. It should have been him, not them.

~

"Are you sure we can't go back to the house?"

It was the fifth time she'd asked him the question as she tossed restlessly on the top bunk. He answered her mechanically, his mind on other things.

"We can't go to your house, Lexi. It wouldn't be safe."

"You can't be sure of that. Why would they leave anyone there, when they had every reason to think we were heading to New York? It doesn't make sense."

She was right. There was very little chance White had bothered leaving men at her house, or near it, on surveillance duty. Very little chance. But a chance, all the same. It would only take them being spotted once to bring White right back to their doorstep. And Romano didn't want the bastard here.

Not yet, anyway.

He'd discovered that he would prefer to have that deadly formula safely on its way to Darren first. Moreover, he admitted, he'd like it if he could get Lexi Stoltz out of the line of fire before it came down to the final confrontation. He didn't want her to see him kill or be killed. She was too damned softhearted to take it.

"Romano?"

"Hmm?"

"I hate calling you that. When are you going to tell me your given name?"

"Don't hold your breath." She could get it out of him, if she applied herself. He figured there wasn't much he could keep from her if she wanted to know bad enough. Things had a way of just slipping out when she was around. She ought to work for the FBI.

"Do you really think there are men watching my house?" She leaned over the edge of the bed so she could see him on the bunk below her. Her hair hung straight down toward the floor and her eyes glimmered in the lamplight. "And tell me the truth, will you?"

"You look like a troll upside down."

"A troll?" Her brows drew together.

"Don't tell me you've never seen *Trolls*. They have long hair that stands straight up in neon colors. Jack must've made me watch that movie about thirty times …"

It had happened again. For just a second, he'd seen his little boy in his mind's eye, sitting in the middle of the living room floor with his troll collection spread out around him, moving the figures around while watching the movie.

He'd remembered. Without effort, his mind had given him a memory and no tidal wave of guilt and pain had come surging in to drown him.

Twice now in one night. Why? Why now? What did it mean?

She was staring at him. Hanging upside down with her troll hair so long he could have reached out and touched it. She was seeing the emotions cross his face, he knew she was.

"Oh," she said softly. Then louder. "Oh, *those* trolls. With the neon-colored hair. I'm not taking that as a compliment, Romano."

Her eyes said more. They touched his soul, those huge brown eyes. They moved over his face and it seemed as if they smoothed some invisible balm over his deepest wounds. He could see the warmth in them. He could feel the healing power of their touch.

She spoke volumes with her eyes. And he heard her.

"But this troll talk is off the subject," she said.

"I suppose it is." His voice came out slow, lazy. He had to shake himself before he could remember what they'd been talking about initially. When it came back to him, he blinked, breaking the grip of her gaze, breaking the spell she'd been putting him under. "Lexi, why are you so determined to go back to the house, anyway?"

"Why are you so determined not to let me?"

"Because it's risky."

"The risk has to be minimal. At least admit that much. There's very little chance White left anyone there and you know it."

He chewed his lip and nodded. "You're right, there's very little chance. But that's still a chance and it's a chance I'm not willing to take."

"We could at least *look*, couldn't we? I mean, if we head over there at night, sneak a look at the house from the woods, we could see for ourselves if there's anyone around."

He propped himself up on one elbow. "This is about that cat of yours, isn't it?"

Her face was turning pink. She nodded upside down.

"Your blood's rushing to your head, Lexi. And if you think I'm gonna risk everything for a cat, it must be interfering with your ability to reason."

She pulled her head up, but a second later her legs hung over the side. Bare feet and smooth calves. And then she hopped to the floor, pacing. "He has to be fed, or he'll die."

"He'll catch a mouse."

"I don't have mice."

"A bird, then."

"But he was shut in!"

"Uh, no. We left a window open."

"A second story window. He's not a flying cat, you know."

"We left that rope ladder. He can climb down that if he gets desperate."

"He's not that kind of a cat."

"I didn't know there was more than one kind," he said.

"Well, there are. There are the lean, nimble, athletic cats and then there are cats like Jax. Round, lazy, spoiled cats who prefer being pampered to hunting big game. He needs me."

She paced to the little stove and set a kettle of water on the burner, then rummaged in the cupboards.

"Lexi, it's only been two days."

She located the box of hot cocoa mix he'd bought, opened a packet and poured it into a disposable cup. Her back was to him. She wore a T-shirt and, as far as he could tell, nothing else.

She looked toward him, tried for a smile, but it was crooked and endearingly sad. "You want a cup?"

"He'll be okay for a little bit longer. The good thing about a cat like Jax is that it can last forty-eight hours without food and probably not even feel hungry."

She nodded. "Maybe."

"We'll get your father's papers from McManus tomorrow. We'll get that formula into the right hands. After that it won't matter."

Her brows bunched together. "There is no formula," she said, her voice a little stiffer than before. But it sounded to Romano as if she was mainly saying it to convince herself. She tore open a second envelope, dumped it into a second cup, then poured the hot water. "And even if there was, what difference will it make? White will still come after us if we're seen up here, won't he?"

"Yes, he'll still come after us."

She stirred the cocoa, carried a cup in each hand and sat down on the edge of his bed. He sat up, taking his cocoa from her hand, touching her fingers as he did so, wishing he hadn't.

"But I'll make sure you—*and* your cat—are someplace safe by then. When White gets here, there's only going to be one person waiting for him."

She held her cup between her hands, her eyes probing his. "You're going to kill him, aren't you?"

He didn't nod, didn't answer. Just averted his gaze and sipped from his cup.

"What if he kills you, instead?"

"He already did that." Damn, there he went again, blurting things that were none of her business. He took another drink, set the cup on the floor.

"He killed your family," she whispered. "But not you. You're still alive."

"My body is, Lexi. That's all, though. There's nothing left inside."

"There is." She put her cup on the floor, not having taken a single sip of the liquid it held. He shook his head in denial, but she caught his face between her palms, held it still, staring so deeply he felt her touch in his soul. "There is, Romano. I see it, right there in your eyes."

"No—"

"You don't want to be alive anymore, because it hurts. You wish it had been you. But it wasn't you. It was them, and they're gone, and it's horrible and unfair. But they wouldn't want you to stay dead inside. They'd want you to go on. Do your grieving and miss them and love them always. But go on."

His hands rose, closing over hers on his face. He moved them away slowly, and he shook with emotion. "I can't do that," he whispered roughly.

"You can, if you just—"

"You don't understand, dammit!" His words exploded from his chest, vibrating through the small camper, making Lexi jerk in surprise. He released her hands, clasped her shoulders, his fingers sinking into her flesh. "It's my fault they died. I screwed up. I underestimated that bastard, and he killed them. He killed Wendy and he killed my boys because of me." He released her suddenly, shoving her away from him as he did. He'd had no choice, because he'd been damn close to clinging to her and letting the magic in those brown eyes heal him.

He no longer doubted that it could.

She scrambled off the bed, and he didn't want her coming back to him. If she touched him again, he'd do something stupid. He turned onto his side, facing the wall.

Lexi stayed where she was. "It wasn't your fault."

"It was."

"Why?"

He closed his eyes. He did not talk about this. Not to anyone. He never had. And he wasn't about to begin now.

And even as he assured himself of those things, the entire ugly story was taking shape in his mind, readying itself to be told. To be shared. With her.

He rolled onto his back, looked up into her brown eyes. He reached out to take hold of her hand, and he pulled her until she sat on the edge of the bunk beside him.

"There was a bomb threat phoned in. That's how it started," he began.

CHAPTER TEN

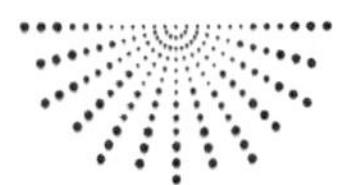

Lexi listened to him talk for a long time. It was as if the floodgates had broken, as if once he started, he had to tell all of it, right to the end. He told her about his last conversation with his wife Wendy, and how Darren, his boss and best friend, had stood by him afterward. Darren had never doubted him, even when his one-time friend, an agent named Stryker, had suspected him of being involved in the murder of his own family.

She'd stretched out on the bunk beside him at some point, laid her head on his pillow. "How could this Stryker person possibly have suspected you?" she whispered.

"The obvious reasons. It was a bomb. They're my specialty."

"But your own family …"

He stroked her hair, and she realized that she now lay in the crook of his arm with her head on his chest and her arm around his waist.

"Stryker knew Wendy and I only married because of the pregnancy."

"You didn't love her?"

"I did," he said quickly. "Just not the way ..." His words trailed off, and he tried again. "We were friends, good friends. Things got out of hand once, when we were both feeling lonely and drinking a little too much. Wendy got pregnant. So we got married."

"But it was working out," she guessed.

"Yeah. Kids have a way of bringing people closer. Two years in, we decided to give Justin a sibling, and Jackson came. It's hard to explain it ... but you'll know what I mean someday when you have children of your own."

That hurt. It hurt beyond belief, but she swallowed the pain, fought it into submission. Talking would do Romano a world of good. She wasn't about to change the subject.

"How did Stryker know about how things were between you and your wife?" she asked, genuinely curious.

"He was in love with Wendy himself. Hell, sometimes I thought she might have wished she'd married him." He lowered his head, hiding whatever crossed his face.

Lexi couldn't imagine any woman falling for another man if Romano was the competition.

"She never said so, though. Never did a thing to make me think that." His voice was sleepy. Long pauses came between his words. "She was too kind to risk hurting me ... and she was loyal." His hand stilled on her hair. "A lot like you," he said. It was almost a whisper.

The last pause drew out. In a few minutes, she realized he'd fallen asleep. Exhausted maybe, from the sudden release of such long pent-up emotions. A soul-deep sleep, she could tell. His chest expanded, lifting her head with his deep inhales.

She sat up, staring down at his relaxed face. "The only person to blame for what happened is White," she whispered. "You did your job. You did what you were supposed to do." Maybe he'd hear her whispers. Maybe they'd get through. "Your family's at peace. You're the only one in hell. You need to see that."

His eyes were still closed, his breathing deep and even. He slept as if comatose, and she thought it was his body's response to the emotional stress of sharing his past—the past that had almost destroyed him.

Lexi didn't imagine he'd ever released any of the rage he'd been feeling over the murder of his wife and little boys. Maybe he'd never talked about it before.

But he had now. And she was glad.

She slipped silently away from him, pausing to pull the covers over his still body. She ached for what he was going through, but she also knew that his past was coloring his judgment of the present. There was no danger in going to the house. There were no men hiding there waiting for her return. Not when White believed they were in New York right now. Even Romano had admitted the chances of such a thing were slim. But he was being overly cautious.

And it would be kind of ignorant of her to think any of that caution was personal. It was fear of failure that made him so careful. He was afraid another death would be added to his list of imaginary sins. He was afraid of what that would do to his soul and maybe even to his mind.

But there was no danger.

She needed to go home, and her reasons went way beyond her desire to make sure Jax was all right. Although, her cat was among the top three.

Romano wouldn't understand any of those reasons. She wasn't sure she understood them herself, entirely. But she had to go back. There were some things she needed to think through and she couldn't do that here, with this wounded hero and his pain so close, so reachable.

She had things to work out, things about herself and her relationship with her father. Things she hadn't wanted to delve into before, because they were too painful. But it was time, she realized. It was past time. And the only place she could analyze and dissect those things was back there at the house where they'd spent the last days of his life together. The place where her memories of her mother shone most brightly. The place that had become her haven and her heart. And of course, there was Jax.

She closed her eyes and turned away from Romano, silently apologizing for what she was about to do. But she wouldn't be gone long enough for him to wake up and worry. She was just going to get close enough to the house to assure herself no one was there. A ten- or fifteen-minute walk. And in the morning, she'd tell him what she'd done, and what she'd found, and he'd stop being so stubborn about going there.

Hell, who was she kidding? If it looked safe, she was at least going to feed her poor cat. And scoop the litter box. And make sure he was warm and safe. And maybe pet him for a little while.

She guessed she'd better leave Romano a note, just in case he woke before she returned. She scribbled on a scrap of paper and left it on the little table.

Making barely a sound, she picked up her clothes. She pulled on a pair of the heavy socks he'd bought, and then one of the sweatshirts. She added one of the heavyweight hoodies he'd found at Walmart, too, and then topped that with his jacket. She took the flashlight, as well.

On tiptoe, she slipped into the front of the RV and then out the front passenger door, rather than using the one in the back, where he'd be more likely to hear or feel the blast of wintry air on his face. She climbed down, into a surprising depth of fresh snow, and closed the door with extreme care, wincing at the noise when it latched.

And then she stepped away from the camper, stretching her arms out to her sides and inhaling deeply of the clean night air.

Snow fell softly but thickly, dusting her face and clothes. It was colder than it had been earlier. Quite a lot colder. It wouldn't be a problem, though. She could find the house blindfolded.

She took a step, then stopped, blinking at the unfamiliar surge of feeling that last thought had evoked. She felt strong and sure of herself, far more so than she had felt before her adventure with Romano. The time she'd spent with him had changed her in a significant way. It had awakened something in her.

She glanced back at the camper, remembering the way he'd looked lying there, asleep and drained, and even a little vulnerable. She thought she was changing him, too.

Romano dreamed of his sons. Jack was playing in a square patch of grass, his cherub cheeks bathed in golden sunlight. Justin was running around him, arms out, making airplane noises, swooping and diving at his little brother and making him giggle even harder. He heard their laughter, saw the sparkle in their eyes.

Then he saw himself and the vision became a memory. He was running and the boys got up and ran with him. He'd been teaching them how to play football in the back yard, the weekend before …

He stopped thinking and just looked, watched the scene unfold in his mind's eye and devoured every second of it. It had been so long since he'd been able to see the boys like this, alive and happy. So long since he'd been capable of or willing to remember, because the pain of remembering was more than he could bear. He'd kept the memories buried, sealed. But now, it was like being there again. So real. The redness of Justin's plump cheeks and little Jack's cupid's bow lips, and the way the wind ruffled their dark curls. The comic size of a regulation football when clutched in the small hands of a four-year-old.

"Boys, time to come in."

He turned at the sound of Wendy's voice. She stood at the back door, smiling as the kids ran toward her, both begging to stay out just a little longer. It was such a familiar scene, one that had played out a thousand times in real life. But it didn't have the feel of a memory anymore.

Smiling, Wendy granted them an extra half hour in the back yard. They raced back to their game, and automatically Romano started toward the back door. He had to talk to Wendy. There was something …

"You called them inside," he said.

"They asked for more time."

"Yeah." Romano smiled. "They always ask for more time."

"And I always give it to them."

He started up the back steps to go inside. He could smell the lasagna baking in the oven. Wendy caught his gaze and shook her head. "You need to wake up now."

He frowned, saying nothing, just staring, confused.

"It was my time, not yours," she said softly. "And it's not Lexi's time yet, either. She needs you. *They* need you."

He tried to argue, but when he opened his mouth, the words that came out had no form, no substance.

"It was my time, not yours," Wendy repeated. "Accept it, and go on."

And then it was as if the lights went out. Blackness descended, engulfing everything. He couldn't see Wendy anymore, or the house, or the yard. He couldn't hear the voices of his sons. There was only darkness, and the unearthly howl of the wind.

It took a full minute for Romano to realize that his eyes were open. He was awake in a pitch-black camper. It had been a dream, for God's sake. Just a dream.

He sat up in bed, pushing his hands through his hair, gnawing his lower lip a little, just to be sure he was really awake.

Seemed he was. And his first instinct was to call to Lexi. To hear her voice answering him would be reassuring. It would confirm everything was all right. Just as it should be.

She needs you.

He gave his head a shake, trying to rid himself of the haunting memory of that dream. It had been so real. He cleared his throat and very softly, not wanting to wake her, he said, "Lexi? You awake?" He waited, remembering with a flush of embarrassment the way he'd poured his heart out to her earlier. The way she'd held him as he'd told her everything. Every single thing he'd vowed not to talk about with another living soul. And how deeply she'd listened. And how sharing it with her had made him feel like maybe he could survive this hell after all.

There was no answer. Okay, so she was asleep. He shouldn't feel such an intense need to hear her voice, anyway. It was ridiculous. As ridiculous as the crushing disappointment of falling asleep with her in his arms, then waking up to find her gone.

She needs you!

Romano rolled his eyes at his own apparent mental instability. But he decided there was no use fighting it. He got out of bed, reached for the gas lamp nearest him and turned the knob. The flame grew brighter, reaching its yellow fingers into the corners, chasing shadows away.

He stood up and turned toward the bunks. He'd just look at her, assure himself that she was okay, and maybe he'd be able to get some sleep.

Only, she wasn't there. The bunk was empty. The sight of it was like a blow between the eyes and he took an involuntary step backward at its impact.

He swore, then checked the bathroom, and swore some more. The camper was as empty as her bed. And her shoes and jeans were gone, and so were the jacket and the flashlight.

"Dammit, she's gone to the house." The note on the table confirmed his suspicion, when he finally noticed it there.

I'm hiking to the house just to take a look. Be right back. Promise.

Okay, okay, calm down, he told himself. So, she'd sneaked out while he slept. So, she'd done exactly what he'd told her not to do. So what? It didn't mean the world was going to end.

He gathered his clothes, picked up his gun. She'd been right from the beginning. There was barely a snowball's chance in hell that White had left men behind to watch her place. She'd be all right. She'd be fine.

He squinted through the RV's windshield, frowning. And then he reached past the steering wheel to turn on the headlights.

But even their blazing white glow couldn't penetrate the blizzard blanketing the night. He couldn't see a yard in front of the RV. Not a yard. Sometime while he'd been sleeping, a brutal wind and blinding snowstorm had kicked up. And Lexi was out there somewhere. A chill of foreboding slipped up his spine, and again he heard his dead wife's meaning-laden whisper. *She needs you.*

He swore. It couldn't have been this bad when she'd left. Couldn't have been, or she wouldn't have gone. Lexi was too smart for that. This was the Adirondack forest, for God's sake. She wouldn't have gone out there alone in a storm like this. He hoped she'd reached the house safely before the blizzard had unleashed its fury, and that no one had been there waiting for her when she had.

He pulled on every sweatshirt that remained, including one of the new hoodies, and fished her pills out of the glove compartment in case she needed them. Then he picked up his duffel bag. Hunching forward, he headed out into the storm.

Lexi made it halfway, she figured, before the snow began flying horizontally instead of vertically, driven by an ever-strengthening, frigid wind. She lost her bearings. It was ridiculous. Stupid, to get lost in a place she knew so well. All she had to do was follow the fire trail, for God's sake. Problem was, she could no longer *see* the fire trail, and the flashlight she gripped was a joke against the power of the sudden storm. When she'd left the camper, it had been cold, yes, but not like this. Now there was a bitter, harsh wind that turned wet snowflakes into razors. There was no light, no darkness. Just snow. She couldn't even make out the shapes of the trees she moved among, until she was nearly inhaling their bark. There was nothing to guide her. The wind moaning eerily through the boughs overhead seemed like the voice of her father. Condemning. Scornful just as he'd always been.

Yes. He had been. Unreasonably, miserably hateful toward her, even before the dementia had set in.

All her life, really. She'd never admitted that to herself before. Down deep, she realized that she'd always thought of herself as unworthy of him. Everyone said he was a great man. She heard it all the time, saw proof of it in the awards and certificates that had lined their home during the height of his career. He'd invented vaccines that had saved countless lives. He was practically a god. To a child, a great man who hated her was proof she was not good enough.

But the truth was, he was just a mean bastard to her for no reason at all.

Her nose and cheeks burned, razed by the blizzard's claws. It hurt to inhale the frigid air, and her lungs screamed with every breath. She felt her heart trip over itself and begin to gallop. The cold and the fear tried to send her into tachycardia, but Lexi fought it. She forced herself to remain calm and tried to take slow, deep breaths. She ordered her body not to betray her now.

She'd left her meds in the camper.

Her hands were wet and slowly going numb, and her feet had long since mutated into solid ice chunks. She couldn't feel them anymore when she stepped on them, so she lurched along, trying to find her way.

But there was no more sign of the fire trail, and she wasn't sure whether she'd have known it even if she'd somehow stumbled onto it again. She only knew she wasn't on the trail now. Somehow she'd veered into the forest. That was obvious by the trees that loomed into her vision with every few steps, towering, but too far apart to provide sufficient shelter from the wind-driven snow. Panic chilled her even more deeply than the cold. But she fought it. There had to be a way to get through this.

She squinted in the snow, trying to see something that would give her a clue which way to go, and finally decided to backtrack. She might be able to find her way back to the fire trail, or maybe all the way to the camper if she just followed her own tracks. Turning in place, she aimed the flashlight at the ground, searching for the footprints she'd left in the snow. She had to bend almost double and hold the light only inches above the ground to see them. Loose snow swirled and whipped around her lower legs like the ghostly mist in a horror movie. Only more deadly. She finally found a shallow indentation in the snow that marked the place where she'd stepped. Then another. Slowly she started back.

She was shivering now. Shaking so hard her teeth rattled and her muscles burned and the flashlight beam jerked and danced in crazy patterns. She pulled her hands up into the sleeves of Romano's jacket, wrapped her arms around herself, huddled into the hood, and bent into the wind that screamed in her ears.

But in only a few yards, the footprints vanished. The blizzard had already filled them in. And now just what on earth was she going to do?

Keep moving. Just keep moving, Lexi, or you'll die out here.

She tried to obey the voice of reason, did for a while. Until it became impossible. The tachycardia came on full force. Her breathing quickened because her brain wasn't receiving enough oxygen. She gasped, sucking breaths of freezing air into her lungs, but she knew it wasn't enough to sustain her. It wasn't that she wasn't breathing in enough, it was that her heart wasn't pumping it efficiently.

Dizziness came as she'd known it would. She groped for a support, her hand sweeping through the falling snow, finding nothing to grasp. She'd only passed out from one of these attacks once in her life. But she knew she was very close to making it twice. And then the snowy ground reached up to surround her face. Its cold was an icy slap, an injection of awareness. She managed to pull herself up again. But her rally didn't last. She staggered forward a few more steps only to collapse against the skin-scraping bark of a massive pine. Her stinging face pressed to the trunk, she tasted its fragrance with every breath.

Romano knew which way she would have gone. He left the headlights on, which would help for a little while. As soon as he stepped out of the camper, the cold bit right through every layer of clothing he wore. Damn. It was frigid, killing cold, with this wind behind it. She wouldn't last long in cold like this. No one would.

He thought about her episodes, the way her heart could take off and that it was sometimes triggered by fear. She'd be afraid right now, if she was out in this storm. If she was lost, she'd be terrified.

Romano snapped himself out of his worry by mentally insisting she'd made it to the house. She was inside right now, and she was warm and dry and safe. He envisioned her wrapped in a blanket, warming her feet by the fireplace, that fat yellow cat purring in her lap.

Only the ever-growing knot in the pit of his stomach kept insisting that wasn't the scene he was going to find.

He managed to stay on the fire trail. He was snow-covered and shivering before he'd reached what he judged was the halfway point, but the extreme cold only drove him on. Maybe he even picked up his pace, calling her name as he went. It seemed that the storm abated a little. That the wind eased and the snowfall slowed as he moved on. Or maybe he was just going numb and his senses were dulled.

But no. He'd made it.

He stopped and stared off into the gloom at his right. There was a glow, very pale, but there. It was like trying to see a streetlight through heavy fog, as he squinted and started toward it. The light led him off the fire trail, into the forest, but it remained visible, even grew clearer as he went. And then the trees he'd been hiking through came to an end. And he was seeing Lexi's house beyond the veil of the storm, the outdoor light glowing like a beacon, and he ran toward it.

Thank God! If the light was on, she must be ...

Halfway across the driveway, he paused, studying that outdoor light now that it was more visible. It was the kind of light that came on automatically at dark.

He put his observational skills into gear and felt his heart sink. There wasn't a single light glowing from inside the house. Only the automatic outdoor one.

He wanted to run up the front steps, slam the door open and yell her name. But he didn't. A lifetime of caution wasn't overcome that easily. He drew the gun and moved slowly, his feet making furrows in the snow. Then he walked up the three concrete steps. He stood before the dark wood door with its fan-shaped, snow-encrusted panes of glass, and he listened.

The house was silent. Not a sound or a movement from within. He didn't think Lexi was there, and the idea that she wasn't almost put him on his knees. They actually began to buckle. It was a sensation Romano had only experienced once in his life.

He steadied himself, trying to weigh his options. Fortunately, it didn't look as if anyone else was there, either. He tucked the gun under his arm and rubbed his hands together to warm them. It didn't help much. Neither did blowing on them.

He turned to look behind him, just once. Just to be sure. No vehicles. No tire tracks. No footprints. Then again, if there had been any, they'd have been filled in by now.

He tried the brass doorknob and found it unlocked. Then he pulled the gun out again with his right hand, held its barrel steady as he opened the door with his left.

In the bit of light that spilled in from outside, he saw the far wall. The dark, empty fireplace without so much as a glowing ember to attest to recent use. No one waited in ambush inside. So Lexi had been right and he'd been overly cautious. No one was there.

Including her.

He replaced the gun and turned on some of the lights. The more light, the better. He didn't care who else might see them right now. These were for Lexi, in case he couldn't find her, the lights might guide her in.

But he would find her. He had to.

He turned back to the door and headed out. He kept thinking of Lexi, lying in the snow, dying. He kept picturing himself discovering her lifeless body, and it was tearing his insides apart. Dammit, she hadn't done a thing to deserve any of this. She'd been dragged into a situation beyond her control, and now she might die because of it.

No. No, she damn well wouldn't die, because he wouldn't let

her. He was going to do it right this time. He wasn't going to lose another person he cared about. Not again.

He swallowed hard, realizing that he'd just admitted he cared for Lexi Stoltz. He hadn't wanted to. But the woman made it impossible to keep a distance. She'd wormed her way under his skin, and yes, he'd let himself care.

She was out there, somewhere. He wasn't going to quit until he found her.

CHAPTER ELEVEN

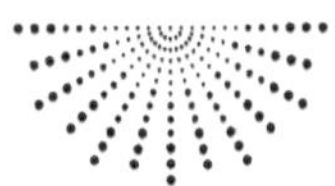

He thought she was dead when he finally found her. He'd been veering into the woods along either side of the fire trail, checking out every snow-covered clump of deadfall that even remotely resembled a body. And then he'd glimpsed a light in the distance and raced toward it. The flashlight was wedged between the limbs of a pine tree, just about head height, aimed back toward the trail. And Lexi lay still at the base of that same tree, snow covering her face and clothes, even her closed eyes, like some morbid white shroud.

His heart did things he hadn't thought it was still capable of doing. Like breaking, for instance. The sight of her shattered it to dust.

He dropped to his knees beside her, choking on the words he tried to shout at her, brushing the snow and frozen hair away from her face and eyelashes. "Lexi! Wake up, Lexi. Come on!" He pressed his nearly numb fingers to her throat in search of a pulse. It wasn't hard to find, because it was pounding like a jackhammer.

"You're alive!" He fumbled in his pockets for her pills, shook two of the tiny tablets from the bottle and then opened her mouth and poked them all the way to the back of her throat, hoping she'd swallow. Then he pulled her limp body against him. Her arms and head hung like a rag doll's, but he held her all the same. "You're alive, and dammit, you're gonna stay that way."

It was closer to the house than back to the camper. Just because White's men hadn't been there when he'd checked the place, didn't mean they weren't watching from somewhere else, or checking in on occasion. But he had no choice, at the moment. Lexi's life hung in the balance.

He lifted her into his arms and began trudging back the way he'd come. She didn't move or make a sound, but he couldn't stop to check her, didn't dare stop to check her, terrified beyond reason that he'd find her heart had stopped.

She wasn't gasping. He told himself her muscles would relax when she was unconscious and that her racing heart might slow down. He looked down at her as he carried her into the pool of light outside the house. Her skin was pale, her frozen lashes resting on her cheeks. She looked like an icy angel, a frozen princess under an evil spell.

He shouldered the door open, kicking it closed behind him, and headed straight up the stairs to her bedroom. Damn, it was cold in there. A little warmer than outside, though. At least there was no wind.

The window was closed. The rope ladder, rolled up and lying neatly beneath it.

That was … bizarre.

He lowered Lexi onto the bed, and pressed his head against her breast to listen. Her heart was beating more slowly than before. Maybe it was back to normal. Maybe she was going to be okay.

She might not stay that way long if he didn't act fast. The hearth in the corner seemed to whisper an answer to him. Kindling laid ready, just as it had when they'd left the house. A stack of wood stood neatly to one side. It only took a second to find the matches on the mantel and light the fire in the fireplace. So he did that, then closed the bedroom door, to keep the heat inside, but just before it closed all the way, the cat rocketed through, leaped onto the bed and bunted Lexi's face with his head.

Romano returned to the bed. Her clothes were wet, frozen. So were his. He needed to warm her, and he needed to do it fast. He quickly stripped to his shorts. Then kneeling on the bed, he took off the coat, then the sweatshirt she wore beneath it. She didn't move as he worked, didn't make a sound, just lay there limp. Lifeless. His throat tried to close off, and his eyes burned inexplicably.

The zipper of her jeans was caked with snow and ice, but he finally managed to undo them. He knelt beside the bed, wrenching the snow-coated shoes from her feet, peeling the socks and then the jeans away. Her skin was cold, clammy to the touch. He hoped to God he'd found her in time. He had to pick her up again to tug back the covers, and then he tucked her beneath them. He wanted to crawl in with her, hold her and rock her and speak to her until he drew some kind of response. But not yet. He quickly searched the room, taking every blanket he found and spreading them over her.

Still shirtless, he ran into the adjoining bathroom, the room where he'd sat on that tiny vanity stool while she'd tended his bleeding shoulder. He snatched several thick towels from the shelf and returned to the fire. He added more logs and then held two of the towels as close to the flames as he dared, warming them. When they were heated through, he went to the foot of the bed, lifted the covers and wrapped a towel around each of her icy feet. He repeated the process with two more towels, wrapping her hands this time.

Then finally, he got beneath the covers with Lexi. She was so cold after the heat of the fire that he flinched and sucked air through his teeth as he pulled her chilled body into his arms and held her tight against his own warm skin. The cat meowed his irritation at having his position disrupted, but settled down again on Lexi's other side, purring loudly.

Gently Romano cradled her, willing his body's heat to move into hers, to warm her, to bring her back.

"Come on, Lexi," he whispered, the harsh desperation in his voice making it sound like someone else's. "Come on, wake up. You're gonna be okay. Do you hear me? You're gonna be okay."

God, if only he could be sure of that.

She was warm again.

It was the first sensation to filter into her awareness. She was warm, deliriously warm and wrapped in a wonderful contrast of hardness and softness. She inhaled nasally, and her eyes opened at the familiar, subtle scent.

Romano.

He was behind her and beneath her and surrounding her. His body enveloped hers in its warmth. She closed her eyes, wondering if this was a dream or some fantasy-based afterlife. Oh, but it felt good, whatever it was. His arms, holding her, warming her, his chest, pressed to her back, his thigh, resting atop her legs, his breath warm on her nape.

She sighed deeply, hoping to stay just like this for several more hours.

He was naked. And … and so was she. No, she realized. Not quite naked. She wore her bra and panties. He wore his boxers.

Lexi came more thoroughly awake. Had something happened between them? Had they slept together and had she somehow managed to forget?

The last thing she remembered was clinging to a pine tree's

rough trunk, shivering with cold and teetering on the brink of unconsciousness.

Romano must have found her. He must have found her and brought her ... She blinked at the windows with their serene blue drapes and rope tiebacks. She sniffed the air, smelling wood smoke and man. She felt the deep rumbling purr of her cat, and his weight, familiar on her pillow.

He'd brought her home. She was in her own bed. And she was all right. She was warm and dry and safe.

Romano had saved her life tonight.

She rolled onto her back, better to see him in the dim predawn light beaming through the windows. He stirred. His eyes opened slow, blinked a couple times, then darted rapidly over her face.

"Lexi ...?"

"I'm okay."

His eyes continued their search, filled with relief. One hand came up from under the covers, to cup her cheek, run through her hair, trace the curve of her neck, as his head moved very slightly from side to side.

"I'm okay," she repeated, knowing he wasn't as sure of it as she was.

He closed his eyes, pulling her closer to him, hugging her tight. "Thank God," he said. "I was afraid ..."

He stopped then. His hands had been sliding down over her back to pull her closer, and they'd paused on her buttocks. His hips were pressed to hers, and she felt the unmistakable swelling of him against her. She lifted her chin, meeting his eyes, knowing he was going to draw away from her at any second, just by the hint of panic she saw in those midnight blue depths.

But she saw desire, too. And she didn't want him to pull away.

She didn't have to move much at all to press her mouth to his.

He shuddered. His entire body trembled, but he didn't turn away. His lips parted when she nudged them. He lay very still, allowing her to kiss him. To taste his mouth. He didn't move when her hands kneaded his shoulders, or when her fingers threaded into his hair.

It was an instinct as old as time that made her hips arch against him. And it was then he came alive.

He rolled her onto her back and urged her lips wider, his tongue digging deep. She felt his body grow hotter, heard the rasping of his breaths. And she knew, without being told, that it had been a long time for him. Longer for her, though. Far longer for her.

He moved his hands between them, to cup her breasts. She stiffened, a little afraid of what was happening.

He lifted his head very slightly, his fevered eyes probing hers. "I'll stop," he rasped. "If you want me to stop, I'll—"

"No," she whispered. "I'm fine, and I want you. I need you."

"I think I might need you, too," he said. And then he resumed kissing her, stroking her, touching her everywhere, until she was sure she'd die if he didn't make love to her soon.

There was fire in his eyes as he covered her body with his, and yet he was gentle. His hands crept beneath her hips, and he held her tight to him, and he made love to her. And it was that, making love. Not just sex. But emotional, exquisite, healing lovemaking. She felt it in every part of her. It was in his tenderness, his superhuman restraint, his every gentle touch.

They moved together, in a dance that melded them as one. Her pleasure built until she was no longer a sentient being, but purely a feeling one. And he kept stoking the flames with every movement, every tender touch of his lips along her jawline, over her neck. He played her like the most fragile instrument, until she reached a shattering crescendo.

He held her as she pulsed around him, her entire body alive and awake and in ecstasy.

And then he moved a little faster, and joined her there.

When he sank to the mattress beside her, never letting her bear his full weight, he pulled her back into his arms, and cradled her there, his powerful heartbeat strong and steady beneath her head. And she knew right then that she loved him. Somehow, she had fallen in love with this tortured, wounded soul.

And so she had to heal him. She had to.

Romano looked at her, lying there with the cold morning sunbathing her naked shoulders, painting the soft smile she wore even in her sleep. The cat had curled up near her head again, sleeping and purring and apparently not half-starved as she'd feared he would be.

He'd done something idiotic. He'd had sex with Lexi. And she was going to think it meant more than it did. More than it could. One look at that soft smile was all it took to confirm that. She'd think it had been some kind of fate thing. But she'd be wrong. His heart had been blown to microscopic bits by one of White's bombs, and Humpty Dumpty stood a better chance of healing than he did.

She stirred a little, snuggling closer to him, one arm wrapping around his waist. Thick black lashes whispered open, and huge dark eyes gazed up at him. The image of the timid woodland creature was back. Only this time it wasn't wary. It was trusting and content.

He was the animal here. He'd used her like a toy, and now he had to make that clear to her. He had to wipe that damned smile off her face before...

Before what, Romano? Before it gets to you?

His throat went dry, and he heard someone whisper, "I'm not ready for this sort of thing."

"Hmm?" she asked.

The way she asked it made "hmm?" sound erotic. And it wasn't *until* she asked it that he realized he'd spoken aloud.

"Nothing."

She bent her head to kiss his chest. Romano slid to the far side of the bed. Finally her dazzled expression cleared a little, and she looked at him, waiting, and he knew that she knew what was coming.

"Is something wrong?" she asked slowly, her probing eyes like pins, pricking him everywhere they landed.

"No. It's just …" He shook his head, looked around the room for a metaphoric hiding place. "I need to throw some more wood on the fire."

"No, you don't." She sat up, leaning her back against the headboard and tugging the covers up with her. "I get the feeling you have something to say, and I think your first three words are going to be 'about last night.'"

Romano sat on the edge of the bed, looking with regret at the soggy ball of denim on the floor. What the hell was he supposed to wear?

"We had sex. What's there to talk about?" This as he got out of the warm bed, wincing at the cool floor against his bare feet. He pulled on his shorts, then hunkered down in front of the fireplace and made a huge production out of poking the coals and arranging more wood atop them.

"Just sex," she said softly.

"Yeah." *Coward, keeping your back to her while you deliver the blow.* "Yeah, Lexi, just sex. I was relieved you weren't dead, and I think you were too. We're both adults."

She was silent. He was afraid to look at her. Afraid he'd see tears in her eyes, and afraid of what that would feel like. He didn't want to hurt her. Better she understand things now, though, than to let her get any crazy ideas about—

The impact of an unidentified projectile against the back of his head cut his thoughts in half. "Ow!"

He turned, rubbing his head with one hand, holding up the other when he saw another book coming at him. Hardcover, too. She couldn't have thrown a paperback?

The second volley ricocheted off his forearm to land on the floor. He eyed the lead crystal lamp on the bedside stand and tried to judge the distance to the door. She didn't reach for it, though. She just sat there, glaring at him as if she'd like to see him beheaded. She didn't say one word. And he didn't ask.

"I … uh … I guess I'll go check on the furnace. It should be running, shouldn't it?"

Nothing. Only blazing eyes as he backed out of the room, into the freezing hallway in nothing but a pair of boxers.

Lexi blinked at the books lying on the floor with their pages folded under them like broken wings. She'd thrown them at him. She tilted her head to one side. Why?

A short time ago, she would have reacted quite differently. She'd have been hurt, yes. But she'd probably have accepted his rejection. She might even have considered it inevitable.

Not now, though. Without thinking it through, she'd reacted with an anger unlike anything she'd ever experienced in her life. A moment ago she'd been mad enough to seriously hurt Romano. Because he'd taken advantage. He'd hurt her, and dammit, she wasn't going to put up with that.

She blinked down her surprise, and turned the idea over and over in her mind. Her outlook had changed in the few days she'd spent with him.

A pathetic wail interrupted her thoughts, and Jax butted her in the chin. "Poor kitty," she said softly, petting him. But he swatted her hand.

"Men," she muttered. "I know, you're hungry. I'm on it." She got up, snatching a bathrobe from the back of a chair and shrugging into it before Jax leapt into her arms. He nudged her chin with his big head and emitted a purr like a race car, punctuated intermittently by meows.

"Poor boy. You've been neglected, haven't you? At least those brutes didn't hurt you." Without using her hands, which were full of yellow cat, she stepped into slippers and headed downstairs. Jax brushed his head over the collar of her robe and against her cheek. She ran her hand over his fur and he arched to her touch, complaining loudly if she dared to stop stroking him for a second.

She was stepping softly, almost on tiptoe, as she descended the stairs. She realized as she crossed the living room that she was *sneaking* through her own house, just because she didn't want to run into Romano again.

Why?

Damn him for making her feel this way. She was bubbling over with the things she wanted to say to him. The problem was, she wasn't sure what those things were. If she opened her mouth right now, she had no idea what sorts of emotional declarations might come out. She was furious with him for the callous way he'd acted. The raw intensity of her emotions frightened her. She'd wait until she was calmer, clearer, before she tried to voice them.

She shivered as she scraped cat food from a can into Jax's empty dish. He dove into the food eagerly. Lexi turned to the sink to rinse the can, and was brought up short when she saw two other cans sitting there, empty, but rinsed.

She was sure she hadn't left them there, and couldn't imagine any of Mr. White's terrorist thugs would have bothered to feed her cat. How odd. She turned on the faucet, but nothing came out.

"The pipes are frozen," Romano said from behind her.

She stiffened at the gruff sound of his voice, but didn't turn to face him. Instead, she shrugged and opened the refrigerator, taking out the milk and pouring a little into Jax's water dish.

"Are you all right?" he asked.

She set the bowl of milk into the microwave, closed the door, hit the 30 second button. "Why wouldn't I be?"

He didn't reply. The microwave hummed as seconds ticked by on the digital panel and the timer beeped. She tested the milk with her forefinger before setting it on the floor. Jax dove into it, tail straight in the air.

"You spoil that cat."

"So did someone else."

"What do you mean?"

"Someone fed him while I was away," she said, nodding at the two empty cans on the side of the sink.

"Someone pulled up the rope ladder and closed your bedroom window, too," he said. "Maybe someone else was looking for you. Any friends or relatives who might've stopped by?"

"I don't have any friends, and certainly no relatives."

She finally turned around, out of excuses to keep her back to him. Then she blinked. Romano wore a pair of her father's trousers, olive drab, with grass stains on the knees.

He plucked at the front of the sweater he'd donned. "My clothes are still wet. I hope it's okay that I borrowed some of your father's."

"They fit you." She blinked again, looking him up and down, almost laughing at the bitter irony. "I guess I shouldn't be surprised, should I? You have so much in common."

She saw his frown, saw his lips part as if to ask her to explain that remark, or to deny it. But he seemed to think better of it.

"I probably should have said something before, but the furnace has been broken since October. I've been meaning to get it fixed, but—"

"Listen."

She tilted her head, and in a moment realized the ancient oil burner in the basement was running. She lifted her brows in surprise.

"The nozzle was clogged," he told her, as if she'd know exactly what that meant. "It just needed cleaning."

"That's good. When the basement warms up, the pipes will probably thaw on their own."

"Not that it matters," Romano said slowly. "We're not staying."

"Maybe *you're* not staying," she replied. "But I am."

"Lexi, just because no one is here now doesn't mean they aren't watching the place. They might check in from time to time."

She shrugged. "I'm staying. I need to be here right now."

He frowned until his brows touched. "Why the hell do you need to be here?"

"I don't know yet." She looked at the way her hands were clasped together, wringing each other, and made them stop, bringing them deliberately down to her sides. "I just feel I have to be here. And nothing you can say is going to make me leave. If you want to go, go by yourself."

"You know damned well I can't leave you here alone."

"Why not, Romano? Why the hell not?"

"Because you could end up dead."

"That would be a real strong argument, except that it's my life. My choice. Not yours. You don't honestly give a damn anyway, so you have no say in what happens to me." She strode past him, heading for the stairway, wanting only to go back up to her warm bedroom and put on her heaviest sweater. She was halfway up the stairs when his voice came from the bottom, stopping her.

"My full name is Connor Lionel Romano," he said, and his voice was very low, very soft. "And I give considerably more than a damn what happens to you."

A tremor ran up her spine, and she closed her eyes as all the air left her lungs. "I wasn't trying to force you to say that," she whispered, knowing that was exactly what she'd been trying to do, consciously or not.

"I know."

She turned slowly, met his eyes, saw the turmoil in them. This wasn't easy for him. He was hurting. It was palpable, his pain. He was almost writhing with it, and she wanted to ease it for him. She offered him a smile that felt weak, and lifted her brows. "Connor Lionel, huh?"

His lips turned up a little at the corners, and the confusion in his eyes cleared. "Yeah. And that's the last time I want to hear you say it."

"All right ... Connor Lionel." She turned around and continued up the stairs. Romano followed. She went back into the bedroom, rubbing her arms and hurrying to stand close to the fireplace. He came in behind her, but she noticed his hesitation in the doorway.

God, he really was scared to death of her, wasn't he?

After a moment's apparent indecision he came inside and closed the door.

"You, uh ... you can bring the cat, if you want," he said, coming to stand beside her. Not too close beside her. Not even close enough.

She realized with a little surprise that she wanted to be close to him, close enough to feel his body heat and hear the pounding of his heart. She wanted to be wrapped up in his arms.

"Bring the cat where?"

"To the camper." He glanced down at her with a wary frown.

"I told you, I'm not going back to the camper."

He swore a long stream, turning in a slow circle, ruffling his hair with one hand. "I thought we settled this."

"We didn't settle anything. I said I was staying here and I meant it."

"And what about White's thugs?"

"What *about* them? They'll find us just as quickly if we leave. There's no way we can get out of here without leaving clear tracks in that new snow out there, unless you sprouted wings overnight."

He opened his mouth. Then he closed it again. Finally, he lifted his hands, palms up. "Okay. All right. We'll stay."

Lexi felt her brows shoot upward in surprise. She tilted her head, questioning him without a word.

"When you're right, Lexi, you're right. We're staying."

She smiled fully.

And he smiled, too, as if he knew every thought that went through her mind. So she held his gaze, and she thought about the way it felt when he kissed her, when he touched her. His smile faded, and his gaze dipped lower, skimming over her neck and down the front of her robe.

"It's cold," he said. "Why don't you get dressed while I try to find something for breakfast?"

CHAPTER TWELVE

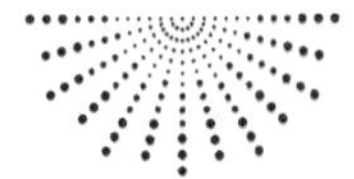

He wanted.

It had been a very long time since he'd *wanted* like this. Every time she looked at him with those big brown eyes, he had to fight the urge to pull her into his arms. He wanted to hold her very close, very gently, and rock her and warm her, and whisper soft words into her ears. He wanted to kiss her. At the oddest moments, for no apparent reason, he kept wanting to cover her moist, warm lips with his. He was craving her taste. He'd never experienced feelings this intense. Not ever. And he didn't want to experience them now.

Dammit, I'm not ready!

Hell, there was no use dwelling on this now, anyway. There was one thing in his future, and only one thing. The capture and execution of White. Romano had nothing to lose. That was his biggest advantage. He wouldn't be able to pull this thing off if that was no longer the case. Nothing to lose meant nothing he wouldn't do. Nothing he wouldn't give up. Nothing he wouldn't risk to get the bastard. It was his mission in life, his one chance to make up for letting his family down. He might end up in prison because of it. He might end up dead because of it. But that was a price he was willing to pay.

Already his determination was compromised. He was not willing to risk Lexi's life to get to White. Which was why he had to get that formula and get her the hell out of here before White showed up.

By late afternoon the house was warm and the water was running again. From the looks of the robin's-egg sky and blinding end-of-day sunlight slanting low, he figured the main roads would soon be cleared, if they weren't already. No plows had passed Lexi's cabin, though. Not all day. Still, the main roads would be fine by now. If the lawyer was coming home today, he'd be able to get through. And if he wasn't, Romano could make his way back to the man's basement office.

He sat on a cream-colored settee with scrolled hardwood arms and legs, near the window, drinking coffee. Lexi came in and sat beside him, and he almost slipped his arm around her shoulders, like it was natural. Like they were a couple. His body seemed to function on autopilot when she got near him. It had all these impulses that just came without consulting his brain for permission.

"I don't think I thanked you for coming after me last night," she said. "I can't imagine how you managed to carry me all the way back here. Your shoulder hasn't even healed from that gunshot wound."

His shoulder. Funny, how he hadn't given it a second thought last night. It ached now, and common sense said it must have been hurting then. But he'd been too focused on Lexi to notice.

"Thank you, Connor. You saved my life."

He liked it better when she called him by his last name. It was less personal. "You can thank me by promising not to leave me like that again." He blinked twice. The words hadn't come out the way he'd intended. "I mean—"

"I promise."

Intense, those eyes. And she was reading more into this whole thing than there was.

"It's about time I head out," he managed to say, thinking it a good idea to change the subject. "Maybe McManus is home by now. I'll take you to the camper, get you settled in there before I go on into town."

"You're going alone?"

He nodded. "After last night— after you almost froze to death in the woods last night, I mean—I don't think hiking down this mountain is exactly what you ought to be doing."

"Jim won't give you my father's things if I'm not there." She sipped her coffee and a tendril of steam rose in front of her face. "Besides, we don't have to walk."

"I know you have a car in the garage," he told her. "I saw it out there the first night. But even if White's thugs didn't do something to disable it before they broke in that first time, we couldn't drive through all this snow."

She smiled mysteriously. "We don't have to walk."

"What are we gonna do, Lexi? I still haven't sprouted wings, and I don't see any sled dogs nearby."

"Sled. No dogs." She laughed and Romano went silent, just listening. He loved to hear her laugh. Her voice was like smoke when she spoke, but it became a drugging smoke when she laughed. Entrancing. Mesmerizing. The fragrant smoke of enchanted incense. Her eyes added to the magic by lighting when she smiled. He liked that. And he liked the way the dimple in her left cheek seemed to wink at him, and ...

I'm not ready for this.

Right.

She lowered her head, and a dark wavy lock fell across her cheek. He tucked it behind her ear. The feat was accomplished before he remembered to tell himself not to do that. She looked up again, still smiling.

"There's a snowmobile in the shed. And we have gasoline stored out there, too. We won't need to walk into town."

"Oh." It was all he could think of to say.

"So can I go with you?"

He was nodding before he could stop himself. And the next thing he knew, Lexi was in the hall closet, pulling out heavy coats and boots and mittens and a couple of plaid woolen scarfs. "Helmets are in the shed, with the machine," she told him.

Romano nodded. He had a small bag of his own packed and waiting near the door. Things he'd need if it turned out the lawyer hadn't returned yet. Some of it from the duffel, other stuff scavenged from around the house. He ought to be thinking about how he would handle that eventuality, because there was no question Lexi would argue.

She'd changed. Right before his eyes, in just a couple of days, she'd changed. There was something … that core of strength he'd sensed in her from the start, maybe. It wasn't so deeply buried anymore. She didn't have to fight so hard to find it now.

Apparently brushes with death agreed with the lady.

He realized he was standing still, staring at her, with what had to be a silly smile on his face.

It was no wonder she'd stayed up here, Lexi thought, as she watched the last traces of the red-orange sun blazing from the horizon under a cloudless, multihued sky. It would be dark soon. The snowmobile sped over the snow, zipping easily under pines with limbs drooping from the weight of the snow. It was beautiful here. Before, she'd seen it as a refuge. A place where she could hide from life and its frequent disappointments. Tonight, she was beginning to see the truly breathtaking beauty around her.

Maybe because of the company.

She tightened her arms around Connor's waist, figuring she might as well take advantage of the current excuse to hold him. He was tense and tightly strung. More now than he had been before they'd made love. She hoped that was because he couldn't deal with his feelings, and not because he didn't have any. She had no idea how to act toward him now.

He seemed to want to pretend last night had never happened. She couldn't forget it even if she tried. She was in love with Connor Romano. And she was afraid of that. Because it would be just like her to love another man who couldn't love in return. First her father. Now Connor. What was the matter with her?

He maneuvered the snowmobile through the forest, and then over the fire trail, then veered off it before they got anywhere near the camper, and cut through the forest down to the road that led into Pine Lake. As he drove, fine white powder rose in an arch behind them, and ice-cold air chilled her right through the heavy gear she wore. At least her face was protected behind the helmet's visor.

In the distance, a huge white circle stood out amid the snowy trees. The lake for which the town was named, almost completely frozen. Then the tiny village loomed into view ahead. When they came to Jim McManus's house, there still wasn't a sign of anyone there.

Lexi's heart fell when Connor pulled in anyway, driving the snowmobile around to the back before killing the engine. He tugged off his helmet. Lexi dismounted the machine and removed her own.

"I don't think they're back yet."

"I think you're right," he said. He swung a leg over the machine and got off, then lifted the seat and pulled a little canvas bag from underneath. "As usual."

He started for the house and Lexi hurried to keep up. "What are you going to do?"

"Something you're not gonna like." He stopped at the back entrance, opened the storm door and tried the next one. "Locked." Opening the bag he'd brought along, he pulled two pointy things out and inserted them into the keyhole.

"Connor!" Her whisper was loud and insistent. "You can't just break in."

He glanced over his shoulder at her, eyebrows dancing up and down. "I just did." He opened the door and stepped inside without a sign of remorse. His form was swallowed by the darkness. There was a soft click, and then the glow of his flashlight. "Come on, Lexi. We don't have all night."

She hesitated in the doorway, gnawing her lower lip. A "snap" broke the silence of the night like a gunshot, and she spun around. Squinting, she scanned the back yard from one side to the other. The rising moon's light made everything clear, right up to the tree line. She couldn't see a thing beyond those first few trees. Standing motionless, she listened, waited. Goose bumps rose on her flesh when she saw something move. Her breath whooshed out of her when she realized it was a pine bough swaying in the wind. But what was that noise?

"Probably just an animal. A deer or something," she assured herself, remembering the deer she and Connor had seen before. And their snowball fight. And she felt warm and safe again.

Squaring her shoulders in resolve, she stepped inside and closed the door.

"Here." Connor pressed the flashlight into her hands. "Lead me to the office."

"It's in the basement." She bit her lip. "There's a separate entrance. I should have told you—"

"I saw it already. This was the easiest lock. Lead on."

Lexi made her way through the kitchen, feeling like a thief in the night, which was exactly what she was, come to think of it.

"Here," she said when they reached the basement door, and

she pushed it open. She took a step downward, only to gasp in surprise when Connor's arm snagged her waist.

"Easy," he whispered. "I don't want you to fall."

She closed her eyes, resisting the impulse to lean back against him, or tip her head sideways so she could press her ear to those lips whispering so close. Instead, she took a deep breath and moved on. More slowly now, though. And instead of worrying about being guilty of breaking and entering, she was wondering why he'd be so concerned about her falling if he didn't care about her. And wondering if he felt the same chills and tingles of awareness that she did whenever they touched.

She reached the bottom. He let go of her. Her disappointed sigh was involuntary, and he couldn't have missed it. He was still too close. She turned left at the base of the stairs, moving the flashlight's beam around until it landed on the office door.

"That's it."

He went to the door, tried the knob. "Shine the light on the lock."

She did. This time he didn't bother with the tools. A simple credit card maneuver that even she was familiar with, and the door surrendered as the first one had. It swung slowly into darkness even more inky than that filling the rest of the house.

"There are no windows in here. You can safely turn the light on."

He did, filling the square oak-paneled office in light. "That helps." Then he turned slowly, scanning the desk's many coffee stains and uneven stacks of envelopes and scattered notes on scraps of paper. He turned to the filing cabinet and pulled a drawer open. "Hey, what do you know? Unlocked. Let's see, Smith, Stanton, there we are, Stoltz, Elliot." The file folder slid from the drawer with an ominous hiss.

Lexi stiffened, wondering if its contents would shatter everything she'd ever believed about her father. Or vindicate him, as she'd been insisting all along they would.

Connor set the folder on the desk and, to her surprise, stepped away. She looked up and met his steady gaze. "Go ahead," he told her. "He was your father. You have every right to look first."

Nodding, she pulled out the desk chair and sat down. Then, hands trembling, she flipped open the folder. Her father's will sat on top. Beneath that, the letter he'd left behind describing the funeral arrangements he preferred. The cremation. She flipped more pages, found more papers and finally came to a copy of the one she'd signed, giving Jim McManus permission to retrieve the contents of the safe-deposit box for her. There was a handwritten note on the bottom. It said simply, "Safe."

She read the word aloud, lifting her head slowly, turning it until she met Connor's eager stare.

He frowned. "Safe?"

She nodded, lifting the paper to him, showing him the notation. Connor scanned the room, stopping when his gaze fell on a painting of dogs playing poker on the wall to the left. He went to it and lifted it down, revealing the small wall safe the painting had been concealing.

"Oh." If the single word conveyed a wealth of disappointment, it was no wonder. Lexi had been hoping to find the truth once and for all tonight. "I guess we're out of luck."

"Sweetheart," he said, and there was a gleam in his eyes. "You're forgetting how I got my nickname."

She widened her eyes and leapt to her feet. "You *can't*—"

"I won't hurt anything but the safe, and we'll reimburse him for that."

She shook her head. "No. Absolutely not."

"Come on, Lexi. What's more important? Finding and ending a WMD that could wipe out millions, or the chance we might mess up some lawyer's office?" He pulled a roll of duct tape and a plastic grocery bag from his duffle, then stood up on a chair to cover the smoke detector with them.

"It's just not ..." She'd been turning in a circle out of sheer frustration as she spoke, and then she stopped. "Look! The light on the answering machine is blinking."

"So?"

"Well, if we listen to the messages, we might find out they're on their way home right now. We might find out they'll be here later tonight or early tomorrow. And if that's the case, we don't really need to do this." She turned to face him, lifting her hands. "Do we?"

He grimaced. His chin fell to his chest. But he got off his chair, reached past her, and pressed the playback button.

Beep.

"Hi, Grandma! Hi, Grandpa!" said the child's voice, bubbling with excitement. "Mommy says we're coming to visit you for Christmas!"

"Ah, God ..." Connor gripped the edge of the desk as if he'd sink to the floor without it.

The little voice went on, but Lexi hit the button to stop it. Then she turned to him, clasped his shoulders and searched his tormented face. "I'm sorry. Are you all right?"

His face was a grimace of agony, eyes closed tightly, lips thin and pale. "I will be," he whispered. "Just as soon as I kill that murdering bastard."

She took a step closer, hearing pain beyond the anger in his voice, wanting to hold him, to comfort him. But he turned away from her, opened his canvas bag and dug around inside. Then he was playing with something that looked like clay.

His entire countenance was meant to warn her away. She couldn't reach him in that place where his pain sent him, so she didn't even try.

He pressed his clay stuff to the safe and stuck little probes at the end of some wire, into it. Then he unrolled more wire from a spool as he stepped backward through the room, backing right out the office door, motioning for her to come with him. When she was out, he closed the door with the wire running underneath it. Taking a small, electronic-looking device from his pack, he attached the ends of the wires to it, then held it in one hand. He used his other hand to push her behind him. Then he moved a knob on the device, and there was a firecracker-like pop in the office. It made her jump, but that was all. For a bomb, it hadn't seemed too terrible.

"Stay here."

She did. When he opened the door, she smelled the heat and saw faint tendrils of smoke. He went back inside the office, and a few minutes later, the light went off, and he emerged with his little rucksack, a thick manila envelope, and the flashlight. Behind him she saw the safe neatly closed with the painting once again hanging in front of it. Nothing else was out of place. He'd even uncovered the smoke detector.

He aimed the flashlight's beam on the handwriting across the front of the envelope. "Stoltz."

"This is it," she said, and her mouth went dry.

"Maybe." Connor tucked the envelope inside his coat, reached to take her hand and started up the stairs. "We'll read it when we get back."

Those words filled Lexi's soul with an inexplicable dread.

He didn't just want, anymore. He *needed.* Dammit, when she touched him, she reached past the grief and guilt and bloodstains on his soul. Her very presence soothed the ache. Just looking at her eased the torture he'd lived with since the bombing. And he was getting used to that. He'd almost grabbed her when he'd heard that little boy's voice on the outdated answering machine. He'd almost wrapped his arms around her and buried his face in her hair. Like she was his refuge. Like she could make it all right. Like if he only held her close enough, long enough, he'd find salvation. Redemption.

It was so damned ridiculous it was almost laughable.

Only Romano wasn't laughing. There was no room in his life for anything like this. No room for *her*. Only vengeance. Lexi Stoltz would take up too much space. She'd shove vengeance right out of his soul and fill it with her own brand of goodness instead, if he let her. He knew she would.

He couldn't let that happen. He had to resist with everything in him, and he had to get away from her.

One more night, he vowed. Because tonight he'd find the truth and tonight he'd figure out a way to get Lexi to safety. Far away from him. Then he'd deal with White.

That voice, the precious voice on the answering machine had reminded him why he was here, what his job was. Thank God for that voice.

The house was warm when they returned. He found he was beginning to like the place. Somehow, she'd taken a cold, over-sized log monstrosity and made it cozy. Cheerful. Even comforting. The fireplace was trimmed in darkly stained wood-work. The sofa was an overstuffed teddy bear of brown velour that hugged you when you sat on it. He stood beside her nearly naked Christmas tree, looking out the big windows at the moonlit night. It was too bad he had to keep his priorities in line. He might enjoy spending more time here.

And who the hell was he kidding? It had nothing to do with the house or the setting. It had everything to do with Lexi.

The envelope was clasped in his hands. He tore it open and pulled out a leather-bound book. And when he looked closer, he saw that it was a journal. There was nothing else.

Well, maybe the formula was in the book. He wouldn't give up hope just yet. He opened the cover, then paused, feeling her gaze on him as surely as he would feel her touch.

Lexi stood across the room, near the fire. Her wide brown eyes filled with more fear than he'd ever seen in them.

He closed the cover. "Maybe you ought to read it first." He held it out to her.

She came forward, her legs none too steady, and extended a hand that trembled as it closed on the supple leather. The way she looked at that diary in her hands, he thought she half expected it to grow teeth and bite her arm off.

She dragged her eyes upward, away from the dreaded book, to his face. "I will. Not yet, though."

"Lexi—"

"Please. I need some time."

"We don't *have* time," he told her. Her brown eyes pleaded with him, and his granite heart turned to mush.

"We can't leave until the roads are cleared anyway, can we? We used about all the gas in the snowmobile."

He lowered his head. "They could be cleared momentarily."

"If they are, we'll leave then and I'll read on the way." She sighed heavily. "I've been through more in the past few days than I've had to deal with in a lifetime, Connor. I need a little normalcy to bolster me. I can't just wade into that diary without something. A hot bath. A decent meal. A glass of wine. That's all I'm asking for. Surely we have time for that."

Connor fell into those velvety brown eyes and figured it would be as hard for White to reach them via snow-blocked roads as it would be for them to leave. "Go ahead, get your normalcy fix. The book will wait."

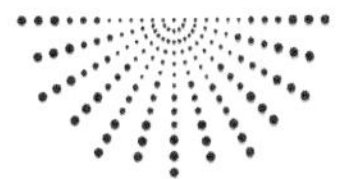

ut that wasn't good enough for her, was it? Oh, no. Not for Lexi Stoltz, the nurturer. The woman who steadfastly defended a father who'd apparently treated her like dirt, and was now soothing the damned soul of a man beyond salvation.

It wasn't enough for her to have her precious normalcy. She had to inflict it on him, as well. And dammit, it was hard enough being near her when people were shooting at them. *This* bull was almost *impossible.*

He was afraid she had a repeat of last night on her mind. But when she came down from her hour-long soak in the tub wearing sweats and a ponytail, he decided that theory might be off the mark. She'd suggested he take a bath, as well, but he'd settled for a quick shower. And when he'd rejoined her there was a fire snapping in the living room hearth. He knew it before he got to the foot of the stairs. He smelled the burning logs, heard the snapping and hissing of the resin.

And he smelled something else, too. Something spicy and Italian that made him hurry his pace. But he slowed it again when he saw the dancing candlelight in the living room. Half a dozen flickering tapers chased shadows up and down the walls.

He lifted his chin, swallowed hard. He didn't want to go to bed with her again. Much as he'd denied it all day long, that first time had damn near shattered his sanity. It had been too intense. Too hot. Too frantic. And just too damned good.

He hadn't stopped thinking about the way it had felt to hold her in his arms since. At least, not until he'd heard that voice on the lawyer's answering machine. That voice had shocked him back to reality the way a pail of ice water would have.

How could he have forgotten so easily in Lexi's arms?

It was wrong. And he wouldn't let it happen again. He had to keep his focus, keep his hatred alive and burning.

She came in from the kitchen with a wineglass full of pale pink liquid in each hand. "Thought you could use a little relaxation, too." She handed him one.

He took it, sipped it.

"Dinner's almost ready. Pasta marinara."

"You waxing domestic on me, Lexi?" His words came out sounding sarcastic and cold. She flinched and her lips thinned. But that wasn't enough for the bastard inside him. "Look, I don't know what you're expecting this to lead to, but it's not gonna be a repeat of last night. It can't be that."

The stricken look in her eyes faded fast. It was replaced by a look of fury. She snatched the wine glass out of his hand and, with a flick of her wrist, applied its contents to his face.

"It's my house. If I feel like cooking, I'll cook. If you don't like it, you can always leave."

Even as the last words left her mouth, she was leaving him there with wine dripping from his chin and burning his eyes. Maybe he was being just a little bit vain to assume seduction was what she had on her mind. But what the hell was he supposed to think?

He played with that idea for a while. Twenty minutes later

she was back, a steaming plate of food in her hand, her wineglass brimming and the bottle tucked under her arm. There was more wine in her glass than there had been before, so she must be on her second. Or third.

She put the plate on the coffee table and sank onto the sofa, curling her legs under her body, drinking deeply from the glass.

"Don't hit the wine too hard. We have to stay sharp."

"You stay sharp," she snapped. "And if you want to eat, do it in the kitchen. I know it'll come as a shock, Romano, but I don't want your company right now."

He rose to the bait, though he should have known better. With a meaningful glance at the firelight and candles, he said, "You could have fooled me."

"The fire and the candles are for my benefit, not yours. They soothe me when things are falling apart. You might recall I had a fire and candles burning that first night you showed up to rain chaos down on my life."

She had a point. There had been candles glowing that night. And she hadn't been seducing anyone then. He took a breath, thinking maybe he'd been mistaken.

"I'm sorry if I jumped to the wrong—"

"I don't think there's anything wrong with me. I really don't." She drained the wine, reached for the bottle, refilled her glass.

"Who said there was anything wrong with you?" She was going to get plastered if she kept it up. Her gaze seemed fixated on the dancing firelight, so he took the bottle and set it on the floor beside the sofa, out of her sight.

"Is there?"

He swallowed hard. She hadn't touched her food. "There's nothing wrong with you."

She met his eyes. She wasn't drunk. If she was, he wouldn't be able to see the hurt in them.

"You lie," she said. "There are lots of things wrong with me. The SVT for starters. And then there's the fact that I can never have children. I don't suppose your background checks on me turned up that little tidbit, did they?"

Connor flinched when she said it.

She shook her head, heaved a long sigh. "This isn't working. I can't relax and pretend things are fine. My brain just isn't buying it." She closed her eyes. "Hand me that stupid book, and then please leave me alone while I read it."

He pursed his lips and finally nodded. He was only just beginning to realize how much she dreaded reading her father's diary. Maybe she sensed something. Maybe … somewhere deep inside her, it was something she'd known for a long time but hadn't acknowledged. Now she'd be forced to see the truth, ready or not.

He should have been a little more understanding.

"Okay." He took the book from the mantel, carried it to the sofa, set it down beside her. She didn't even look at it. "Are you sure you'll be okay alone?"

"I've always been okay alone, Romano."

She'd said to leave her alone. He didn't. Not really. He left for a few minutes, long enough to eat a plateful of food and pour a glass of water, though he was dying to sample that wine *internally*. When he finished, he went very quietly into the big foyer, where the stairs landed. He sat down on the bottom step, his water in his hands, and he watched her.

She read, oblivious to his presence. Her hands trembled a little, then a little more. Blinking as if dazed, she laid the book down, staring straight ahead. What she was seeing, though, wasn't in the living room with her. It was in her mind. And whatever it was, it wasn't pleasant. Not with those tears springing into her eyes. Not with her lower lip quivering that way.

Squeezing her eyes tight, drawing a deep breath, she seemed to gird herself. Then she looked at the pages again, and she read some more.

It was killing him not to go in there. At first, his eagerness had been based on his hope that there would be references to the formula in the diary. But that concern had faded. Now all he wanted to know was what that book could hold that would hurt Lexi like this. Because it *was* hurting her. Pain etched itself more deeply into her eyes with every page she turned. Romano knew pain. He knew it too well not to see it cutting her heart to ribbons.

It was an hour before she stopped reading. She looked shell-shocked when she closed the cover, laid her father's diary on the table and got to her feet. Her knees wobbled, but he was there before she could fall. He grabbed her shoulders, and gazed down at her face. He wanted to hold her. Lord, how he wanted to hold her.

"Let go."

Two words. A harsh whisper wrapped in hurt and anger. He didn't let go. He pulled her to his chest and slid his arms around her. He stroked her hair, wishing he could snap the band that held it captive. "What is it? What did he write that hurt you this bad?"

With anger that surprised him, she pulled free. Her eyes were tear glazed and distant when they met his.

"You don't care. Why are you asking when you know you don't care?"

Romano gave his head a shake. She bent over the coffee table, and when she straightened, she held the diary out to him. "Here. Take it. It's what you came for. It's why you stayed. Take it and read it. Maybe your precious answers are in there. I don't know. I couldn't ... didn't finish it."

"Lexi ..."

She pressed the book into his hands and turned away, her

ponytail snapping with the motion. Romano threw the diary onto the floor. "I don't give a damn about the book right now." He touched her shoulder, and she stopped walking away from him but didn't turn around. "Come on, talk to me. Tell me what's wrong, maybe I can help."

"I don't need your kind of help. Just …" She drew a breath, tears shuddering on its surface like dew on a windblown leaf. "Just leave me alone."

She walked up the stairs. He heard the bedroom door close, and that was all.

"Damn."

His gaze was drawn downward, to the diary on the floor. He could go upstairs after her, but he had a feeling she wouldn't tell him a thing. Or, he could leave her alone as she'd asked and read the book for himself.

He squatted on his haunches and picked it up.

Lexi lay face down on the bed, crying, heartbroken. He'd never loved her. Her father had never loved her.

No. Not her father. He hadn't even *been* her father.

The words he'd scrawled in his poisonous ink about her and her mother were etched indelibly in Lexi's mind.

I couldn't stand the woman. Marrying her was the biggest mistake of my life. And I should have known all along the brat she carried wasn't mine. Five years later, she died, weak, sickly thing that she was, leaving me to raise another man's child.

"All those years," Lexi whispered, and she slowly sat up. She brushed the hot tears with the back of one hand and was surprised when no fresh ones fell to burn her face. "All those years, bending over backwards to please him. But it didn't matter what I did, what I *was*, or what I became. None of it mattered."

Her eyes dried slowly, leaving salt on her skin. "None of it mattered," she said again, and finally it was beginning to sink in. Her eyes were opening. She was understanding. It hadn't been that she unworthy, or that she'd disappointed her genius father in some way. It had never been that. She could have been crowned queen of the world and he still wouldn't have loved her.

"It wasn't me. It was never me, it was him." Pushing both hands through her hair, she sat on the edge of the bed. It wasn't a revelation, though. Not really. It was merely confirmation of something she'd been feeling for a very long time. But she'd been unable to acknowledge it. Because if it were true, then it would mean her father was just a selfish, cruel jerk who was truly unworthy of her love. But he was the only person she could love, the only person in her young life. So rather than face the truth, she'd seen her entire existence through the warped glass of a lie. She'd chosen to believe every adult who ever told her what a great man her father was and how many lives he'd saved. And her mother, who'd told her geniuses were different, and needed to be cared for and protected.

All those things had made her see herself as a warped reflection in a funhouse mirror. She'd let herself feel inadequate, unworthy of the great man's love, when deep down, she'd known better. She'd always known better.

Lexi sniffed and yanked open the drawer in the nightstand. Her scrap book lay there, and she took it out, opened the cover. There she was five years old, getting on the school bus for the first time. The mother of the little boy next door had taken the picture, certainly not her own father. Lexi happened to be in the shot because they got on the bus together. And the woman had sent her son in with a copy for Lexi a week later.

She'd been terrified to get on that big yellow bus. Her father had called her a coward.

"But I wasn't," she whispered, remembering now more

vividly than she ever had before. "That boy … Billy … he was just as scared as I was. But his mother came to the bus with him. She hugged him hard, and promised she'd be waiting right there in the same spot when he came home that afternoon."

The pain in her heart softened then and began to change form, to alter into something else. She flipped the page.

There was the shy little girl in the second-grade production of *The Wizard of Oz.* Only she'd had no proud parent in the audience. Her father had said he might be willing to take the afternoon off if she'd gotten the lead, but he certainly wasn't missing work to see her play an extra.

"I thought if I could only be better … just be better, he'd love me."

The pain became an ember, and as she flipped more pages, relived other disappointments, other times when he'd made her feel worthless, the ember glowed hotter and brighter. It turned out she was capable of feeling anger toward a man she'd adored. She'd *ached* to win his affection. She'd become a doctor to try to earn his love. But he'd never once given it.

"Damn you," she whispered when she flipped a page and found a photo of him, accepting some award. She stood up, tearing the cellophane away, peeling the photo from the book, holding it at arm's length in a white-knuckled grip, and she said it again, louder this time. "Damn you! How could you do that to a motherless child who adored you?"

Rage welled higher, flooding her soul and spilling out of her. It had built up there all her life, but it had been denied. No more. No more.

"It wasn't me, you selfish bastard! Do you hear me? It was never me. It was you!" She flipped pages, tearing out every clipping about one of his achievements, every story about another award he'd won, every article calling him brilliant. "You're the one who wasn't good enough. You didn't deserve the love I lavished on you. And you were wrong to throw it away! You were stupid to throw it away! And so is that idiot downstairs!"

Crumpling the photos and clippings, she took a shuddering breath. She felt strong. She felt free of a terrible burden she'd carried too long.

"I *am* good enough," she told the wad in her hands. "I always was. You were too filled with hate to see it. And Romano is too filled with guilt, and this damned quest for vengeance. I love him. I love him a hundred times more than I ever loved you!" She fell to her knees in front of the hearth, her chin falling to her chest, her eyes filling again. "But he can't return that feeling any more than you could, can he, Father? No, of course he can't. And I'll tell you something, I'm through. I'm not going to waste any more of my heart on men too stupid to know my value. I *am* worthy, dammit. And one of these days, I'll find someone who's worthy *of me.*"

She tossed the wad of keepsakes into the fire. Red flames licked at them, devoured them, turned them into a charred ball of ash, which she thought resembled her father's black soul. "I will," she whispered. "I swear to God, I will."

"Lexi ..."

She stiffened, not turning at the sound of Connor's hoarse voice coming from the bedroom doorway. How long had he been there? How much had he heard?

It didn't matter, did it? She'd made her decision. She thought maybe she was beginning to know herself as she truly was for the very first time.

She got to her feet, choosing to ignore his intrusion. Crossing the bedroom, she opened the closet and located a cardboard box in the back. Bending to it, she flipped it over, emptying its contents onto the floor and tossing the box onto the bed. Then she crossed the room again, her steps fast and sure. She picked up the trophies, the gold watches, the medallions her father had won over the years, and dropped them into the box.

Connor followed her as she moved down the hallway, yanking framed certificates off the walls. He'd hung more every day since they'd arrived. Those went into the box too.

Then she returned to her bedroom, and went to the framed portrait of her father that sat on her nightstand. She threw it at the box as if she were trying to pulverize it. The sound of breaking glass was satisfying.

"I know you're angry," Connor said. "You have every right to be."

She tipped her jewelry box upside down, shaking the contents onto the dresser, shoving the piles around. Her class ring. He'd complained about the cost but finally shelled out the money for it in lieu of a birthday present. It felt hard and cold in her palm, and then it sailed through the air like a missile, the box its target.

"Will you stop? Will you just talk to me for a minute? Please?" He grabbed her arm. "Stop this. Lexi, we have to talk."

She stood still, panting with rage. She couldn't look at him.

He touched her face, lifted her chin, and she met his eyes. "I'm sorry. I don't know what else to say."

She wanted to fold herself into his arms, just melt against his strong chest, and let him rock her, hold her. She wanted that so much!

But she stood still, unblinking. "Did you find what you wanted in the diary?"

He shook his head. "No."

She was tired. Drained. Slowly her taut muscles unclenched, and she managed to stop grinding her teeth and calm her breathing.

"Tell me what other bombshells you found in that damned book," she said, the words falling from her lips without inflection or emotion.

Connor cleared his throat. "He made a deal with a Mr. White to develop the formula in secret, right under the noses of his team at the University. It's all in the diary. He was paid a lot money for it."

Lexi closed her eyes, nodding slowly. "He always complained he was unappreciated. All the acclaim, all the prizes, it was never enough. And the whole time, he wasn't even capable of loyalty to his own country. Or even to mankind."

Swallowing hard, she opened her eyes again, faced Connor's blue ones, wished she didn't see so much concern for her in their depths. "What else?"

He cleared his throat. "He collected half the money up front, and was supposed to get the rest on delivery of the formula. But apparently, he got cold feet."

"Oh?"

"He accidentally exposed himself. Once he realized he was dying, he seemed to find a conscience. Either that, or he wanted time to try to develop a cure. Whatever his reasons, he decided to back out of the deal. He knew White wouldn't take that lying down, so he decided to drop out of sight." Connor watched her face. "For what it's worth, he wrote that he kept himself away from everyone until the incubation period had passed. He knew he was no longer contagious by the time he got near you, or anyone else again."

"The man was a saint," she whispered, remembering the three days he hadn't come home from his lab. That was when she'd begun to suspect dementia.

"The man was a fool."

"So are you." She held his gaze for a long moment. He didn't argue. In fact, he lowered his eyes as if in silent concession.

She swallowed hard, looked away from him. "I'm a doctor. Why didn't I see symptoms of this virus before it killed him?"

"The symptoms were subtle, and he only recognized them himself because of the research he'd been doing. Forgetfulness was one. The rest he could have hidden easily enough. Fatigue. Night sweats. Gradually decline over a six-to-twelve-week period, followed by sudden death."

True, Lexi realized. All true. "Did the diary say what he did with his research or the formula itself?"

Connor shook his head.

She sighed long and low. "That's it, then."

He looked up, met her eyes, his brows raised in question.

"You wasted your time coming up here and dragging me into this whole thing," she said, and she fought to keep her voice level, to sound rational and calm. "And I really think it's time we ended it, don't you?"

"I can't leave. You know that."

She shrugged. "Then I will. You can have the place to yourself, Romano. Tear up the floorboards looking for the formula. I'll come back someday when this is all over." She picked up the box she'd been filling and started for the door.

"You can't just leave!"

He followed her, but she did her best to pretend he wasn't there as she descended the stairs. She carried the box through the foyer and to the back door, then balanced it on her hip while she got the door open. She stepped into a pair of tall rubber boots, and then outside into the frigid air.

Connor grabbed their coats and followed right behind her, yelling questions all the way, but she ignored him. This was between her and her father.

The icy wind stinging her cheeks felt good. It cleared her head, numbed her heart a little to the hurt her false father had inflicted so deeply for so long. She trudged through the snow, across the lawn to the tiny rectangle that had been his garden. And there she tipped the box upside down, spilling its contents onto the snow.

"There you go, Father. You always preferred the company of this stupid patch of dirt to mine. You should have been buried right here. It would have suited you, wouldn't it? No time for a daughter who loved you. No. But plenty of time for all that puttering. Out here all the time, digging. Always digging. That was all you ever ..."

Lexi let her tirade fade to silence, and the cardboard box fell from her hands. She stood there blinking down at the snow around her feet. And just like that, she knew. She simply *knew*.

Without lifting her head or turning to face Connor, she said, "Get a shovel."

CHAPTER FOURTEEN

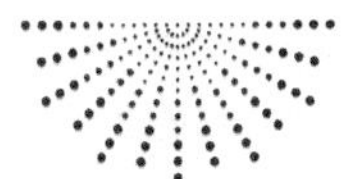

$\mathcal{H}$e ought to be excited, knowing he was so close. But instead, as he poked around the little garden shed with a flashlight in search of a shovel, he was thinking about Lexi. As if getting inside her head—inside her heart—had suddenly become more important than finding the formula. More important than getting White. More important than anything.

Ridiculous. He knew that. But still his mind seemed obsessed with the puzzle of Lexi to the exclusion of anything else. She'd gone from devastation to rage to something else in a matter of minutes. He still hadn't identified the final emotion. The one she'd reached as she'd stormed out into the snow. Acceptance, maybe, and a decision to leave everything behind, including him, and to start fresh somewhere, free of the emotional baggage she'd been lugging around all her life.

He was living proof it wasn't that easy.

Hell, when he'd heard her ranting at her dead father, he'd had no choice but to go to her. He'd wanted to comfort her the way she'd managed to comfort him.

It was true. She *had* comforted him. She'd found a way,

despite his determination not to let her. She'd reached right through his pain and held his frozen heart in her warm hands, thawing it. She'd even begun to heal some of the fractures he'd thought went too deep to mend.

He'd never known anyone who felt things as deeply as Lexi did. To cry so easily for a pain that wasn't even her own … the way she'd cried when he'd told her about his family. And he'd never known anyone with a more soothing way about her. Every time she touched him, even if it was only with her eyes—no, *especially* when it was with her eyes—it felt as if she was healing his deepest wounds.

She deserved better than what her father had given her. And in spite of himself, he knew she deserved better than what *he'd* given her.

Upstairs, when she'd been raging at her dead father, she'd blurted out that she loved him. *Him.* Connor Romano, a man so hollowed-out, there was nothing left but a shell.

Or was there?

He was beginning to think there might be, because he didn't feel like a used-up husk anymore. He felt as if there *was* some spark of life left in him. Maybe he wasn't quite as dead inside as he'd thought.

He located the garden tools, pocketed the flashlight and grabbed a pick and a shovel.

Hell of a time to be thinking this way, Romano. Hell of a time. Because if you dig up what you think you're going to, it's all over. Time to get her as far away from you as possible. Time to deliver the formula to the good guys, and lie in wait for White. Time to exact the punishment he so richly deserves.

There aren't going to be any fairytale endings. Not here. Not now. And not for you, Romano. Never for you.

He dropped the pick and shovel onto the ground outside, half-hoping Lexi was wrong about this, just to prolong his time with her. A stupid thought but an honest one. Maybe the first honest one he'd had in quite a while.

~

She huddled deeper into her parka, wondering how on earth Connor could stand to work with no coat at all. He'd started out with one, but had shrugged it off, warm with the effort of digging ground. He wore a T-shirt and stood in the knee-deep hole he'd dug. Lumpy brown chunks of frosty earth lay scattered around him like cobblestones. He'd put an ugly brown scar in the snow's flawless face.

And then he stopped and said, "I think I found something."

He looked up at her, and the yellow glow of the kerosene lamps she'd brought out, painted his face with light and shadow.

Lexi swallowed the lump in her throat. It wasn't caused by fear of what she might learn about her father. She'd already been dealt that blow. And it had staggered her and hurt her. But she'd survived it. Her heart was sinking now for a far different reason.

They both knew that once the formula was found, their time together would end. Connor hadn't said it out loud, but it was there, real and black and devastating. To her, at least.

She lifted her chin deliberately. "Let's see what it is."

He held her gaze for a long moment, and there was something there in the midnight-blue depths of his eyes, some fire in them that went beyond the lamplight they reflected. Then he dropped to his knees in the frozen dirt. Using the shovel like a whisk broom, he scraped the rest of the dirt away. When he tossed the shovel aside, he worked with his bare hands, digging down along the square outline's edges with his fingers. Lexi picked up the flashlight and aimed it into the hole. He clenched his jaw as he worked a small metal box free of the earth, and picked it up.

He stared at the box while she stared at him. "This is it," he said, his words so soft they were all but lost in the slight breeze that ruffled his sable hair. "It has to be. What else would he bury out here?"

Her throat burned. "There's a padlock."

Connor nodded. "That's easy to fix."

"You're not going to blow it up, are you?"

It should have been funny. He should have laughed and then she should have joined him. But instead he only looked into her eyes with a sad little smile. She wanted to cry.

He set the box down on battered brown earth, reaching for the shovel again. Then he hit the padlock with it until the lock broke free.

And again, he surprised her by seeming more eager to see what was going on in her eyes than what was inside that box.

He paused, searching her face. "You want to go inside for this?"

Inside? Yes, she wanted to go inside. And she wanted to throw herself into his arms and beg him not to open that Pandora's box. Not yet, at least. She wasn't ready to say goodbye.

"No." Oddly enough, her voice gave no indication of her turmoil. "Let's do it right here."

Connor nodded. He worked the misshapen padlock's hasp until it came out and then he opened the box and pulled out a simple spiral notebook, the kind you could pick up at any drugstore for ninety-nine cents. It didn't look capable of destroying the world.

He dropped the box and stepped out of the hole, up onto the level, snowy ground nearer the kerosene lamps she'd lit while he'd been digging. He flipped open the cover. Lexi moved closer. Her flashlight illuminated the white pages, and her eyes scanned line after line of numbers and symbols, some of which she understood, and others she'd never seen before.

She knew enough, though, to realize that this was a formula. A recipe for death, right there, in Connor's strong hands.

"Well. Seems I've arrived just in time."

Lexi gasped, whirling at the grating voice she'd heard only once before. Her surprise at seeing the pale man standing there in the snow paralyzed her for an instant.

Mr. White, the man who'd murdered Connor's wife and little boys, stood too close, his feet planted on either side of the shovel, pointing a gun at them. "I'll take that notebook, Romano."

"The hell you will."

White shook his head, smiling, chilling her with the evil that seemed to glow from his pink eyes whenever he looked at her. "You have two choices. I shoot you and take the book. Or you give me the book—" his grin broadened, "—and *then* I shoot you."

Lexi must have moved, though she wasn't aware of it, because White's alien eyes jerked toward her all of a sudden. "As *for you*, pretty lady, you just stand perfectly still. You surprised me last time, but I won't make that mistake again."

She said a word she'd never uttered in her life as a blinding, white-hot rage exploded in her brain, then lifted her foot and stomped down hard on the business end of the shovel. Its handle shot upward, right between White's legs and he fell to the ground howling.

Only it wasn't just an agonized howl. He was howling ... a name, a command. Connor slammed the notebook into Lexi's chest and jumped on White.

Lights blazed in the distance as some tank-sized pickup truck bounded toward them. Its path vaguely followed that of the dirt road, crushing the snow that covered it. Its spotlight swung left and right, finally stopping when it illuminated the two men tangled in combat, fighting for the gun.

Lexi made a mad dash for the snowmobile they'd left parked

near the front steps. The second she stepped away from their boss, the men in the mutant pickup started shooting at her. Puffs of snow appeared in front of her feet where the bullets hit. She stuffed the journal inside her coat and ran faster. Tires spun in snow as the approaching truck sought traction, then lurched, then spun, then lurched, making its way closer through the deep, unplowed snow.

She swung onto the snowmobile, almost shouting in triumph when it started on the first try. Gunning it, she shot easily over the snow. And when she reached the spot where Connor and White still wrestled for the gun, she jerked the handlebars and hit the brake, skidding around sideways.

"Connor!"

She wasn't even sure he heard her shriek his name. Then he landed a blow to White's chin that snapped the bastard's head backward, shoved himself to his feet, and jumped on behind her. One of his arms wrapped around her waist, and his body bowed over hers, shielding her while she gunned the throttle. They shot off into the forest with bullets zinging after them.

Romano was frozen half to death by the time they reached the little town. Not that it mattered. His shivering was nothing compared to what would happen if White and his goons caught up to them.

Fortunately, by the time the bad guys got that oversized truck turned around and headed back down the mountain, he and Lexi would be long gone.

He and Lexi. He'd thought they'd be going their separate ways. But the bastard had arrived early and ruined his plans.

Why was he so glad about that?

Lexi pulled the machine around behind the general store

and killed the engine. And only then did it occur to him to ask, "Where's the notebook?"

She patted the front of her coat. "Right here. Don't worry."

As she said it, she turned to look at him over her shoulder, and he had to battle the urge to kiss her. And then he asked himself why he had to battle it, and he kissed her anyway.

It was brief. His lips caught hers, drew on them for a moment. He wanted more, but—

"There's a car in that driveway across the street," he said softly.

"Don't tell me. We're going to steal it."

"Borrow it. Come on." He got off the sled, took her hand and together they ran across the road to the car. Connor glanced in through the driver's side window, and smiled when he saw the keys dangling from the switch. "Romano catches a break," he muttered. He nodded to Lexi and she went to the other side.

When he opened his door, she did the same. They landed simultaneously in the front seat, and when the two doors slammed, there was only one bang. They backed out, and started down the road without a single light coming on in a single window.

As they drove farther away and safety seemed within reach, Connor felt like he ought to say something or *do* something to let Lexi know ... *something.*

But what?

That he wanted her to stick around, maybe? Yeah, that he wanted her to stick with him a little longer.

He opened his mouth to try to vocalize that, and he'd already said her name before he realized how stupid it would sound.

He realized something else, too. This wasn't over. And he had no business even thinking about involving her in his future —if, indeed, that *was* where this train of thought was leading— until he knew he had one. The formula wasn't safe yet. Beyond that, White was still breathing. Until he killed the bastard, there was no reason to think about anything else. Because he might very well die trying. And that wouldn't be fair to her.

She was looking at him, waiting for him to finish what he'd started to say. Those big, dark eyes of hers were drinking the heart right out of his body and into her own. She made love to his soul when she looked at him like that. How did she *do* that?

"You were fantastic back there, Lexi. Saved our asses once again."

"I was mad. Too mad to be scared, I guess."

"You were smart. And yeah, mad as well. Too mad to take time to question your own judgment. You trusted your instincts. You ever notice how every time you do that, your instincts turn out to be right on target?"

She smiled at him and his heart stopped. "Yeah. I *have,* actually."

CHAPTER FIFTEEN

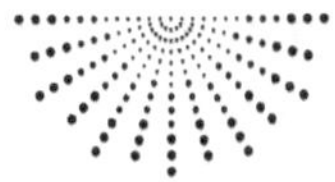

"We've got a hit!" Kira shouted.

The four half-sisters of Lexi Stoltz and their husbands had gathered at Nick and Toni's sprawling Victorian. The women wanted to stick together until they found their missing sister, and the men didn't like being away from their women. Toni's place was the biggest, next to Cait and Dylan's mansion, but that was in Maine, so the upstate New York Victorian it was.

Toni's young sheepdog, Ralph, was delighted by all the company, and had personally slobbered each and every one of them with love.

They'd all been working the case in one way or another, trying to find Lexi and her abductor. Or rescuer. Or whatever former FBI agent Connor "Molotov" Romano was. So it had been busy, and the energy was tense and worried. But in all of that, there'd been beautiful moments. Laughter. Tears. Secrets shared. Trust built.

Everyone gathered around Kira, who was stationed at the kitchen island with her laptop. "They took a flight to Dulles, used their own names."

"What does that mean?" Cait asked. She had the prettiest blue eyes, Kira thought. She hoped Cait's baby had eyes like those. Her niece. Yeah, she was gonna be an auntie this summer. Imagine that. Being Auntie Kira, alongside her sisters, Aunt Toni, Aunt Joey, and if all went well, Aunt Lexi, too.

Toni said, "It might mean they think it's over. That they're safe."

Kira's husband and fellow DEA agent Michael was looking at his phone. "Stryker is in the D.C. office, but says he doesn't know anything more than we do. He hasn't heard from Romano in months."

"We have to go down there," Joey said. "I don't mean we ought to, I mean we *have* to. Lexi needs us."

She wasn't just giving her opinion. She knew something. Kira had left her doubt about the existence of ESP in the dust since spending time with Joey.

"Let's go then," Kira said.

"Caitlin, you should stay here." Toni probably didn't realize she was holding her arm out, kind of crossing it in front of Cait when she said it.

"I'm coming. I won't do anything to put the baby in danger, but I ..." She looked at the others. "I want to be with you guys ... when we find her. I want us to be together."

"Yeah. I get that." Kira looked at the women. Delicate Caity, so obviously from a different world than the rest of them. Born rich, still rich. Like stupid rich, not just well off like Kira's own family. Cait was trying hard to be just one of the girls. But she had the kind of class that showed right through her strategically ripped jeans and button-down boyfriend shirt. Her architect husband Dylan went cow-eyed every time he looked at her.

Joey was funny and smart, and that *thing* she had made her feel like the oddball of the bunch. It was cool, though how everyone accepted her. Besides, it wasn't that weird. She was intuitive. Okay, she was way beyond intuitive. And it *was* a little weird, but she was so much more. She rode a motorcycle every-where she went from May to November. Her husband Ash was a hotshot journalist who'd been a lot of help chasing down leads and sniffing out clues.

Toni was the most like her, Kira thought. And the least. Her kick ass-ness had come from necessity. She had street in her. She'd had to get tough early. Kira wouldn't have wanted to tangle with Toni. Yeah, she was a famous writer. She could walk with the elite. But she wasn't part of them. She was a lioness, walking with the zebras. She knew it, and more importantly, the zebras knew it. Her husband Nick was a cop, and he was almost as hot as Kira's own husband. Toni, clearly thought he was even hotter.

Her sisters, Kira thought. A little while ago, she'd been the most isolated person on the planet. The most alone. She hadn't even had herself.

Now … well … now, just look at this family she'd found.

"We'll all go," Kira said softly. "We can look out for each other, especially our mom-to-be."

"I'll have to find someone to stay with Ralph," Toni said. "But that won't be hard. He has a dog-sitter waiting list."

Connor and Lexi were in a hotel room in Washington D.C. It wasn't where he'd wanted to bring her. Everything in him, every cell in his body was urging him to take her home.

Home, since the explosion that had taken his family, was a houseboat, bobbing serenely off a tiny island in St. Lawrence County, on the New York/Canada border. It was an easy place to isolate himself. But he found he didn't want to be alone anymore. He wanted to be with Lexi.

Hell, that idea had been taking shape in his mind for hours now. He wanted to take her into his home, into his life … and he wanted to ask her to stay. He wanted to tell her that he wasn't sure he could ever be a whole human being again, but being near her made it feel possible.

Maybe it wouldn't be fair to ask her to stick around. He didn't think he'd be able to get past the loss of his little boys. Not ever. There was a huge part of him that had died with Justin and Jackson. He didn't think he'd ever get that part of him back. But there was another part of him, a vital part, that was beginning to heal, and he knew that was because of Lexi. Selfishly, he wanted that healing to go on. He wanted to keep her close. He wanted to try … God, he wanted to try to love her.

Sometime during their flight, he'd seen the possibility of a future for him; a future that included Lexi. It hovered in the distance like a glimmering beacon of light at the end of a black, lifeless tunnel.

That glimpse of light, of hope, had only lasted for a short time. It was shattered when he answered his phone and heard Darren Wade's three clipped words. "White is here."

His grip on the receiver tightened painfully. His gaze followed Lexi as she sat in front of a mirror and ran a brush through her long hair.

"Did you hear what I said, Romano? He's here, in Washington. He must have followed you."

"I hear you, Darren." Romano's voice was strained. He tried clearing his throat while his ideas about trying to make a future for himself and Lexi dissolved like sugar in hot coffee.

"You still have the formula? It's safe and in your possession?"

"I have it." He'd texted his boss as soon as they'd got off the plane to let him know he was back, but no details had been discussed. He'd been waiting for and expecting this call.

"What about the Doctors Stoltz?" Darren went on. "We need to take them into custody, and it—"

"No." At the force he put into the single word, Lexi turned from the mirror to stare at him, searching his face. He shifted in his chair but couldn't break the hold of her gaze. "Elliot Stoltz is dead," he explained, more calmly. "And his daughter had no knowledge of his crimes."

"No investigation. I want it clear, right now, Darren. No charges against Lexi Stoltz. Give me your word, as a friend, or I won't bother bringing in the damned formula at all."

"We shouldn't bring it anyway," Lexi said, loud enough so Darren could hear her too. "We should destroy it."

"Romano, we need the formula in order to create the antidote. We don't know who else might already have it."

"If anyone else had it, White wouldn't be wasting his time chasing me. Anyone else would be an easier target."

"We can't be sure of that." Darren swallowed hard, then took a long, slow breath. "All right, okay. You say the daughter's innocent, she's innocent."

"She is."

Lexi laid her brush on the dresser and stood up. She came to him while Darren was still speaking, and the sight of her slow approach made him lose his hearing for a moment. Darren's voice faded to nothingness as she ran one palm over the side of his face and mouthed the words "thank you," her eyes brimming.

He closed his eyes at the emotions her touch evoked. And even then, couldn't stop himself from turning until his lips touched her palm.

Her smile was tremulous, maybe uncertain. She mouthed the word "Shower," and then went into the bathroom and closed the door.

"—if she's that important to you, you're not going to want her at risk," Darren was saying. "I want her in custody."

Connor shook himself. "Risk of what?"

"Try listening this time, Romano, this is vital. White is here. He obviously knows you still have the formula. He'll try to get to you before you have the chance to turn it in. And that means tonight. We need to take some precautions. If we don't, you and the Stoltz woman might both end up dead, and that formula in the worst possible hands."

It was true. If White was in D.C., then he must be planning another attempt. And he'd kill them outright this time. He wouldn't risk being bested again.

"I can bring it in right now," Connor suggested.

"White knows enough to have the building staked out. He might try to take you before you get inside. But it shouldn't be hard for me to slip out of here unnoticed. You can turn over the formula, and then you and the woman come in with me. We stick you in a safehouse with armed guards—"

"Protective custody." Connor grimaced at the thought.

"Just until we manage to let White know it's too late. We'll try to pick him up before he skips the country again, but this way, even if he gets past us, he'll still have no reason to bother you or the Stoltz woman again. She'll be safe."

"You know what I'm gonna say. You, of all people, Darren, know exactly what my answer is. You know me better than anyone alive." Darren started to speak, but Connor went on. "I'm not coming in."

"Romano—"

"It's not up for debate, Darren. Come to me tonight, and make damn sure you're not followed. I'll give you the formula, and you can take Lexi to a safehouse. Guard her with your life. She means something to me."

Darren hesitated, maybe tripped up by that declaration. Then he said, "Yeah, well, she won't if you're dead."

"We do this my way or no way," Romano told him, keeping his voice level.

"All right. Okay. Go on, what else?"

"That's it. Take her somewhere safe. Get your best guys to work on the antidote and then put that damned formula down the nearest toilet. But don't let it slip that you have it. I want White to think he still has a chance."

"But he'll still come after you if he thinks that." Then he sighed. "That's what you want, isn't it? He'll come after you tonight, and you'll—"

"Better than letting him get away again, don't you think?"

Darren sighed, but didn't argue. "Tell me where you are, my friend."

"Yeah." Romano looked toward the bathroom door, where he could hear the shower running, and he thought of how furious Lexi was going to be with him for this. She wouldn't go willingly. He knew she wouldn't. "Give me a couple of hours, okay?"

"Sure. Whatever you want."

So he told him the name of the hotel and their room number. A few minutes earlier he'd been wondering if he could convince Lexi to stay with him. Now, he was trying to think of a way to convince her to leave.

Connor seemed pensive.

Lexi wanted to know what he was thinking, what he was feeling, but she wouldn't ask. If he had something to say to her, something to tell her, he'd have to do it on his own.

When she came out of the bathroom fresh from a shower, he was pretending to watch television. There was an open pizza box on the table.

His face was expressionless, but there was trouble in his eyes. His shoulders were too stiff, too square.

She'd thought they were safe. They'd left the killers behind, found the formula, brought it to the good guys.

Only they hadn't given it to the good guys just yet. And it was pretty clear that her feeling of finally being safe was an illusion.

"You might as well tell me," she said. "I can see in your face something's wrong."

"Nothing's wrong. This thing is almost over, that's all." He got up from the sofa and came toward her. "You've been great. I couldn't have done it without you."

"I've been fighting you every step of the way." She met his eyes, saw what was in them, and didn't like it a bit.

This was it. He was getting ready to say goodbye.

"Lexi—"

"Don't." She pulled her hand away, a flutter of panic in her chest. Not now. Not yet. But she couldn't keep her eyes away from his if she tried. So much feeling in them. So much emotion. How could he pretend not to have feelings, when his eyes were oceans of them? "You're going to say it's over, aren't you?"

He closed his eyes, nodded slowly.

"And what if I say I don't want it to be?"

"I don't want it to be either." It wasn't the reply she'd expected, and she got the feeling it wasn't the one he'd meant to give. She thought there were tears in his eyes. "I'd like you to stay with me. Live with me. Make love to me every night. I'd like that a lot."

"Then ask me, Connor. Just ask me. We'll get out of here right now, tonight, drop that notebook off with your boss on our way."

A little muscle in his jaw twitched. He averted his eyes, and his next words came as if he were forcing them out. "I can't."

She shoved his chest with both hands, so he stumbled a step or two away from her. "Damn you, Connor Romano! I don't deserve this. You know I don't."

"I know."

"Then tell me why."

Her voice had grown softer, squeezing through a smaller space as her throat tightened. There was regret in his eyes, though, and the anger went out of her, leaving her deflated. She sank into the chair again, out of strength. Her fight was gone. Only heartache and confusion remained. He didn't want to do this, to end what was beginning between them. So why was he?

Connor came around the table, closed his hands on her shoulders. She didn't resist as he pulled her close to him. Her face pressed to his hard belly. "Don't ever think it was you," he whispered. "It's about me."

She swallowed hard, refusing to cry as she pushed away from him. She stood again, her legs wobbling, and she meant to turn away, to put some distance between them, but he kissed her. He kissed her and her insides melted and her mind just emptied. He kissed her with his mouth and with his teeth and with his tongue, and the way he held her made her think he never wanted to let go.

She shook her head, finally managing to take a single step away from him. The air felt cold without his arms around her. "I can't."

"Lexi—"

"No, Connor. If it's over, it's over. I've spent my whole life loving a man who couldn't love me back and I've been repeating the pattern with you. I'm done with that. I deserve … more."

The look that flashed in his eyes could have been pride, but there was pain, too. She saw it very clearly.

"You could love me, you know," she told him. "But you won't let yourself, will you?"

"I …" He couldn't seem to look into her eyes for more than a second. "I'm sorry," he whispered, his voice tortured and coarse.

She took a deep breath, stiffened her spine. "I'm not going to beg." Closing her eyes, searching inside for strength, she forced herself to end this torment, to say the final words, to break free. "I'd like to leave tonight."

He lowered his head in acceptance when what she wanted the idiot to do was beg her to stay.

"That's probably for the best."

So this was it. It was over.

But not my life. My life is just beginning, really.

She was free of a father who'd done nothing but belittle her. She was free of the warped self-image she'd dragged through life like a ball and chain. She was free of the secrets of her birth.

She'd finally discovered the woman she truly was, and she liked that woman. Dr. Lexi Stoltz. Smart, strong, brave, capable of outsmarting international terrorists. She could get through anything.

"Even this," she whispered, and cleared her throat when Connor only frowned at her. "I'll go back to the clinic where I used to work, before all this. For a while anyway. I need to practice medicine again. I didn't realize how much I've missed it."

His head came up. "I'll book a flight out for you. Tomorrow."

She shook her head. "I told you, I want to leave tonight."

He drew a breath, pinned her with his gaze. "You are leaving tonight."

"I don't—"

Her words were cut off by a knock on the door.

Connor stared at her a moment longer, and she saw the anguish in his eyes. Then he turned away, pulled the gun from his waistband, and went to the door. Standing to one side, he asked, "Who is it?"

"Darren," a voice answered.

Connor nodded and opened the door. The man who entered was a head shorter than him and about fifty pounds heavier. His hair stuck up straight in a snowy brush cut and his eyes were baby blue. His first act, after closing the door behind him, was to clasp Connor's hand in both of his. "You look good, my friend. I knew working a case would agree with you."

"I said to give me two hours," Connor said.

"And I said White's in town. Do you want her safe, or don't you?"

Connor nodded, then glanced toward Lexi. She'd been trying to knuckle her eyes dry without being obvious.

"Lexi Stoltz, Darren Wade."

She nodded, muttering hello while searching Connor's face. Something was going on here.

"The formula?" the newcomer asked.

Connor nodded, then got the spiral notebook from where he'd tucked it under the mattress. Lexi couldn't help sucking a breath through her teeth when he handed it over.

The men heard it and he looked at her quickly. "It's okay, Lexi. I trust Darren with my life."

"And have, a time or two," Darren Wade said, and the men exchanged a familiar look. There were a hundred remembered stories in that one look. "It's all right, Miz Stoltz. I know this is difficult. Believe me, you'll be as safe as if you were in your own mother's arms."

She blinked at the reference to her mother, then frowned as the rest of his words sank in. "What do you mean?" Her gaze flicked back to Connor. "What's going on?"

"I want you to go with Darren, Lexi." He put his hands on her shoulders and she got the feeling it was more to make sure she wouldn't run from the room than to comfort or reassure her. "He's taking you to a secure location for the night. By tomorrow it should be safe for you to go home."

She pulled free of his hands, shaking her head. "This doesn't make any sense. It's over now. You gave him the notebook."

"White has no way of knowing that," he said.

She blinked slowly, her mind racing. And then suddenly, she got it. "You don't *want* him to know. You think he's going to come after you tonight, don't you? And you want me out of the way."

Connor said nothing, but he broke eye contact, looking down at the floor. She blinked back tears and went to stand face-to-face with Darren Wade. "If you're really his friend, you won't let him do this. He's not going to arrest White, he's going to execute him or die trying. You can't let him—"

"Now, calm down, Miz Stoltz. Romano isn't gonna do anything foolish. I'm not gonna let him lie in wait all by himself. He'll have backup and plenty of it. White will be arrested and brought to justice."

Dread settled heavy in the pit of her stomach. "Don't do this, Connor."

Darren kept right on talking, as if unaware of the emotional undercurrents snapping in the air.

"Go with him. Lexi, for God's sake, don't make this any harder than it is."

She shook her head. "No."

Darren Wade's fleshy hand closed on her arm gently. "I'm sorry, Miz Stoltz. Try to understand, White's responsible for mass murders, bombings, assassinations, kidnappings. We can't risk him escaping again, no matter what we have to do to prevent it."

She tugged her arm away, annoyed at him getting between her and Connor. "I *said* no."

"I have the authority to arrest you, Miz—"

"It's *Doctor* Stoltz," she snapped, and then her gaze flew to Connor's.

"I'm sorry, Lexi. It's for your own protection."

She looked at him in stark disbelief, and the pain in his eyes almost brought her to her knees. "It's a choice. You know that, don't you? It's a choice between a chance at living again, and your vendetta against White."

He lowered his head. "This is something I have to do."

So he knew. He understood. And he was choosing hatred over love. "Do you know how good it could have been between us?" she whispered. "Do you have any idea what you're throwing away?"

"Yeah." His voice was so choked it was barely audible. "Yeah, I do."

"I was falling in *love* with you."

"Goodbye, Lexi."

His words stung. Tears surged into her eyes, and she bit her lip to stop it from trembling. She didn't have any idea how to fight this, or what she could do to change his mind.

Darren Wade closed the lid and picked up the pizza box. "You're done with this, right?"

Then he patted Lexi's shoulder in a fatherly gesture and keeping it there, steered her out of the room, into the hallway. She held Connor's gaze until they stepped into the elevator, and when the doors slid closed, it felt as if they sliced her heart in half.

CHAPTER SIXTEEN

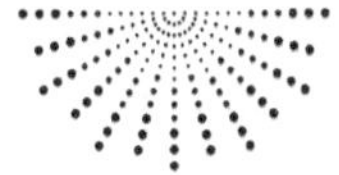

The elevator doors closed, and that was good, because it stopped him from seeing the hurt in Lexi's eyes.

He stepped back into the hotel room, closed the door and a quake moved up through his body. His fist hit the table so hard the plates jumped from the surface, and pain flashed through the wound in his shoulder. He tipped his head backward and battled the acidic burn behind his eyes. He swore at the top of his lungs, berating the ceiling and the walls. And the reason he was punching inanimate objects and swearing a blue streak was because the only alternative would have been to sink to the floor and cry.

He'd known it would be hard. He hadn't realized just how hard, though. He hadn't realized that seeing hurt shimmering in her eyes would make him hate himself. He hadn't expected her to tell him she was falling in love with him.

Was being the operative phrase. He'd ruined it. But ... it would be different, once she realized he was only sending her away for her own safety. Maybe if he survived this, he could find her again, explain to her that he hadn't meant the things he'd said. That he'd hurt her because it was the only way he could be sure she'd go with Darren. Maybe she'd forgive him and understand.

Do you have any idea what you're throwing away?

Romano closed his eyes and sank slowly into a chair as her words came back to him in that smoky voice, made huskier by pain. Who the hell was he kidding? He knew it wouldn't matter if he explained himself. Lexi knew it, too. She was right. He'd made a choice tonight. He could have handed that formula over to Darren, taken Lexi and left, like she said. They could have gone away together. Started over.

But no. He'd chosen to stay here and await his longtime enemy. He'd chosen a man he hated over a woman he …

What?

He didn't know. Maybe now he'd never find out.

He showered, dressed, re-bandaged his shoulder, and cleaned and loaded his weapons while he waited. He knew the drill. By now Lexi was someplace safe, far from here. By now, this hotel had twenty of the Bureau's finest in strategic locations to back him up.

But Connor would get a shot at the man who'd taken his family before this night was over.

He tried to picture White's cold eyes in his mind, but instead he saw Lexi's. Wide and brown and hurt. Those eyes that healed a man just by looking at him. Those beautiful, sexy, mesmerizing eyes.

He laid the gun down on the dresser, closed his eyes, tried to erase the longing for her that grew stronger with every breath, every second. Was this what the rest of his life would be like? Was killing White worth this?

No.

The answer came to him as clearly and precisely as if it had been spoken aloud. No. It was that simple. White would be apprehended if he showed up tonight. It wouldn't matter if Connor was in the room or not. What mattered, what really mattered, was Lexi.

He'd made a choice tonight. The wrong choice.

God, he'd thrown away his last chance at redemption. He'd thrown away a woman unlike any other he'd ever known. Or ever would. Lexi had been falling in love with him. And he'd chased her away.

Was he insane?

But it wasn't over yet. It couldn't be over. Maybe there was still time to make things right.

He tucked his favorite gun into his waistband before pulling on his jacket. It smelled faintly like Lexi's hair. The longing stabbed deeper. He quickened his pace, almost ran through the hall to the elevator and then rode it down to the lobby.

The agents sent to back him up were doing an excellent job of concealing their presence. He didn't see a single face he recognized, nor did anyone look conspicuous.

He headed outside to hail a cab. They backup guys would see him leaving. They'd get the idea. They were skilled enough to be able to handle White on their own. Darren would've sent plenty of firepower. He knew what was at stake. One less agent wouldn't make a difference.

As the hotel faded in the distance behind him, Connor felt lighter, and he couldn't wipe off his stupid grin. He'd made the right decision. Late, but still…

Tension knotted his stomach as he wondered whether Lexi would forgive him for not making it sooner.

The taxi dropped him off outside the government building he'd worked out of for most of his career. He paid the driver and headed inside, only to run smack into Monroe Stryker, who was hurrying out.

"Damn, why don't you watch where you're—" Stryker met

Connor's eyes and stopped in mid-sentence. "Romano. What the hell are you doing here?"

"I know I'm supposed to be at the hotel waiting for White, but I've got to see Lexi."

"What are you talking about?"

"Darren didn't tell you?" At Stryker's blank stare, he went on. "I assumed he'd have brought you in on things now that he has the formula."

Every drop of color left Stryker's face. "Tell me you're not talking about the Stoltz case."

"That's exactly what I'm talking about. Look, I know you still hold me responsible for Wendy's death. I don't blame you. Hell, I wouldn't have done this for Darren at all, if the chance to get White hadn't been a part of it. But it's over. I got the damned formula and turned it in. I did my part. Now I've changed my mind about the protective custody for Lexi. I want her back."

"Protective custody? For Lexia *Stoltz?*"

Connor nodded. "I think I finally understand why you hate my guts so much. If you felt a tenth for Wendy what I feel for Lexi … it's a wonder you didn't put a bullet between my eyes a long time ago."

Stryker gaped, then drew a breath. "I did worse than that to you."

"What?"

He shook his head. "Not now. Look, Romano, you're telling me you went after Stoltz's formula at Darren Wade's request. You turned it over to him, and then you let him take the Dr. Lexia Stoltz into custody?"

"Yeah. For her own protection. I was planning …" Connor swallowed hard. "I was planning to take White out tonight."

Stryker lowered his head into his hands and swore.

A lead ball formed in Connor's stomach. "What the hell is going on?"

"Darren Wade doesn't work for us anymore. For more than a

year now, I've suspected him of selling information. I've been watching him but haven't been able to get anything solid on him. Not yet anyway."

"Selling information … to whom?"

"To White."

The word hit Connor like a blow to the solar plexus.

"I thought you were working with him, Romano. Dammit, you two were best friends. Darren's the one who recruited you. So when it looked like he was involved in the bombing that killed Wendy, I assumed you were in on it, too. Especially since the device was so well made … and so much like White's work. Only you knew his methods that well. And only you had the skill to duplicate them."

Connor swore, but Stryker kept talking.

"I figured Wendy knew something, stumbled onto some information she shouldn't have …" He trailed off, shaking his head.

But Connor wasn't hearing him anymore. He was replaying that last conversation he'd had with his wife. It caught like a scratched LP, skipping back to the same phrase over and over again. *Saw your boss today. Saw your boss today. Saw your boss today.*

"No."

He closed his eyes, gave it a mental kick to make it play out and die away. And then he heard the rest. *He was talking to the oddest looking—oh, hey, Justin's hanging upside down from the monkey bars and hollering at me to come out and see. Gotta go. See you when you get here.*

Only she hadn't. Instead, she'd been killed right before his eyes. Killed because White had planted one of his trademark devices in the house. When he shouldn't even have known where the house was. When he shouldn't have known anything about Connor's family.

So how had he known?

He was talking to the oddest looking ...

"It was Darren," Connor muttered. "Good God, it was Darren all along. Wendy saw him that day, she and the kids ran into him. They said he was with someone odd looking. Had to be White. He and Darren both knew all it would take was one mention of what that stranger looked like for me to put it together ..." His head fell until his chin touched his chest. "Those bastards killed my little boys." He snapped his head up. "Those bastards have Lexi!"

"They also have a virus capable of wiping out entire nations, Romano. We'll get them." Stryker was already pulling out his phone, tapping keys.

Connor was reeling, his mind spinning out of control. "I made her go with him. Dammit, she didn't want to."

"We'll have every resource at our disposal on this within ten minutes," Stryker said. "We'll get the formula, and we'll get Lexia Stoltz." He headed through the doors that led to the street, Connor on his heels. "Park yourself somewhere, Romano. I'll get in touch as soon as we know anything."

"The hell I will. I want in on this. And after what you believed, you owe me that much."

Stryker lowered his gaze, conceding too easily "I owe you a hell of a lot more than that, Romano."

"What's that supposed to mean?"

"I'd like to be alive to close this case," he said. "So I'll explain later. For what it's worth, Romano, I'm sorry." He clapped Connor's shoulder. "Come on. I've got a friend in the CIA who's been tailing Darren for days. Had to keep it out of the house, if you get my drift. And also, you should know your friend Dr. Stoltz has a very worried family trying real hard to track her down."

"She doesn't have any family," he said as they hurried to Stryker's car.

"Yeah, she does. Just doesn't know it yet. You remember Mike Waters?"

"DEA?"

"That's the one. He's her brother-in-law. I'll explain on the way. Come on."

❦

Kira Waters' phone was chirping as soon as she got off the plane at Dulles. So was Michael's. It was a text message from Michael's FBI friend, Stryker, who had cc'd them both. "White has Dr. Stoltz. CALL."

Kira's blood chilled in her veins. Her sisters crowded close to look over her shoulder at the phone.

"Oh God," Cait whispered.

Michael beat Kira to the call button, but she took his phone right out of his hand, hit the speaker icon, and held it outward as the others gathered around.

"Stryker," a man's voice said when he finally picked up.

Kira angled the phone toward her husband. He said, "It's Waters, We're at Dulles and you're on speaker. What can you tell us?"

"I'm with Romano," Stryker said. "He handed Stoltz off to his former boss, Darren Wade. He didn't know Wade wasn't with the Bureau anymore."

"Why not?" Kira asked.

"Wade resigned. I suspected he was in collusion with the international terrorist known as Mr. White."

"Oh my God," Cait said again.

"Why is an international terrorist after our sister?" Toni asked.

Kira shot Michael a look, and he gave a subtle shake of his head. It bothered her not to tell her sisters about the biological weapon Lexi's mad scientist fake-father had created.

Then again, not knowing that would probably let them sleep easier at night.

"Thanks, Stryker," Michael said. "We need to meet up with you, join forces, help with the search."

"You and Kira," Stryker said. "Keep the civilians a safe distance out, all right?"

"All right?" Michael asked, looking at the women.

They exchanged glances, and then all shook their heads left and right.

Raining. Great, Lexi thought. A perfect match for her mood. Snowing up north, probably. Raining here. She thought about commuter flights and ice-coated wings, and wondered if it would stop raining by the time she was free to catch a plane back to New York state. And then she shook her head, knowing it didn't matter. She wasn't going anywhere. Not until she saw Connor again.

She supposed she was a glutton for punishment, but she couldn't just walk away without knowing what happened to him tonight; whether he went through with his plan to kill White; whether he came out of the whole thing in one piece. She had to look into his eyes just once and see that it was really over. Because she hadn't seen that in his eyes tonight. Not at all.

Darren Wade hadn't said a word since they'd got into the car. He'd offered her a slice of pizza, then eaten one himself while driving away from the bustling streets and into more rural areas. She saw the sign when they crossed into Virginia and wondered just how far away this safe place was.

The car continued steadily onward, wipers slapping water from the glass, headlights piercing the gloom. And then he pulled to a stop in front of what looked like an empty warehouse or equipment hangar at the end of a long road through a lot of nothing.

"What is this place?" she asked, squinting through the windshield, trying to make sense of what she saw. Broken windows, sagging roof. "Why are we stopping here?"

Darren didn't turn to face her. Very softly he said, "I'm real sorry about this, Miz Stoltz."

Then her door was yanked open from the outside, letting in a blast of cold, wind-driven rain. The interior lights came on, and they were enough to illuminate the pink eyes and white hair of the man she'd thought she'd only see again in nightmares.

She screamed and kicked him while scrambling backward across the seat. He leaned in, absorbing her kicks like they were nothing. He grabbed her shoulders, his fingers sinking deep, and dragged her out into the frigid, icy rain that pelted her face like shrapnel. He crushed her against his chest, pinning her arms to her sides. She twisted and kicked, but he was oblivious.

"Come on, I don't have all day. The syringe is in my back pocket. Take it and inject her so we can move on with things."

His shrill words terrified her, and she fought harder. Darren's steps slapped the wet ground as he came around the car.

"No, you can't—"

And then the fine, sharp tip of a needle pierced the flesh of her buttocks. The rain grew louder and louder until it enveloped her. And soon she couldn't do anything more than listen. Her body was weak, and seemed to have stopped obeying commands.

White picked her up, draped her over his shoulder, and she felt the cold rain soaking her back but couldn't move to avoid it.

He opened the car door, tossed her across the back seat. "You," he said to someone beyond her sight, "Drive the car inside before it's seen. Secure her but be careful. She's clever.

Bear in mind, I might need her later. Mr. Wade and I have some business to conduct in the office."

She heard whoever it was get in, heard and felt the car door close, and then the vehicle was moving.

"I'm sorry, Monroe," Michael Waters said to Stryker. He was apologizing for the six extra civilians he'd brought with him.

Waters' wife Kira stood beside him on the side of a deserted stretch of road. She wore tall black boots and leather, and she was armed to the teeth. She was also agitated and twitchy.

"Don't apologize," she said. "We're her family, and we can help. Besides, none of us are exactly civilians."

"Look, I specifically said—" Stryker began.

"He's going to kill her," Romano said. "Who the hell cares who's here and who's not? He's going to fucking kill her if we don't find her in time!"

Kira slammed her palm to his chest, just when he'd been about to turn away in frustration, and when he blinked down at her, there was something familiar about her face, the curve of her cheeks, the shape of her nose.

"Who *are* you?" she asked.

"Connor Romano."

"I figured," she said. "Lexia Stoltz is my half-sister. And that piece of shit White is *not* going to kill her."

And then he realized these people were the relatives Stryker had mentioned. "She doesn't know she has a sister."

"She has four of them," Kira said with a loving look at the three other women standing around in the rain, two blondes and a brunette who shared Lexi's coloring, stood nearby.

Stryker looked frustrated and walked away, back to the gathering of agents and state police who'd gathered at this deserted crossroads. Darren's phone had pinged a cell tower nearby. One of the cops had found it in the ditch at a four corners where he'd apparently tossed it.

Romano wished the icy rain could shake the sick feeling from the pit of his stomach. But it didn't. It couldn't. Nothing could. Lexi was still alive, or had been when Darren had run a red light and the traffic-cam had snapped a picture. She'd been sitting in the passenger seat. That should've given him a hint of relief. But it didn't. She was alive, but in the hands of brutal killers because of him. He would get her back or die trying.

Aloud, he only cleared his throat and went over to Stryker. "Where the hell is that chopper you asked for?"

Stryker answered, but Romano was almost beyond hearing. He had no idea where Darren had taken Lexi. But he was afraid she'd be turned over to White along with the formula in short order. Unless he could get to her first.

One of the women in the group, gasped. Kira Waters went over to her, and they spoke quietly. She had a head full of wavy caramel and honey blonde hair, and at the moment her hands were buried in it, as if she had a headache.

In a minute, Kira came to him, took his arm, and led him a little bit away from the others. "She's being held in a large building. It's pre-fab metal, light blue with white doors. The windows are mostly busted out. It's cold."

"How the hell do you know all that?" he asked.

Kira looked at the blonde she'd just spoken to. "Joey saw it. Just … trust me. Go with it."

"There's a map in the car," Mike Waters said, and Kira scrambled into their rental, leaving the door open as she dug through the glove box then unfolded a map over the dashboard. "Stryker said the cell signal stopped moving—" he glanced at his watch. "Seventeen minutes ago. Given the heavy rain, let's estimate a radius of about—"

"Fifteen to twenty miles," Kira said. "Maybe up to twenty-five, but I doubt it." She measured with her finger, then drew a crooked ass circle encompassing the search area. Then she looked up, confidence in her eyes. "How many big blue buildings with white metal doors and busted out windows do you figure there are within that radius?" Then she drew a line through the center of the circle, "And even less if we rule out the ones back in the direction we came from. We're gonna find her."

"We'd better hurry," Romano said. "Once White has the formula, he won't have any reason to keep her alive."

Her back thudded from the car to the floor, then scraped over rough, cold concrete as one of White's lackeys dragged her. She heard voices from some other part of the building, but didn't dare open her eyes to look around.

He let go of her shoulders, and her head dropped onto the floor. She had to clench her jaw to keep from yelping in pain.

"… pay me now," Darren Wade was saying in the distance. "I kept my end of the bargain. You have the formula."

I should've torn those pages out of that notebook and flushed them. I knew I should've. Dammit, why didn't I?

"If it proves to be legitimate." That was White's vibrato voice. "More legitimate than your loyalty."

"What do you mean?"

"Do you really think I don't know what you've been up to? That you've been negotiating with certain … competitors, trying to get a better offer?" White made a little clucking sound with his tongue. "You're a fool, Wade. I know everything you do."

"I did ask around," Darren said. His voice was different. Pitched with fear. "But I didn't go through with it—"

"You might have, though, if I hadn't arrived here and monitored your every move. You've put me to a lot of trouble, you know. All the expense and effort of trying to take the formula from Romano before he turned it over to you, just in case you grew the gonads to betray me."

"None of that matters, now," Darren said, his voice trembling. "I gave the formula to you. You have it in your hands right now."

"Indeed," White said slowly, calmly. "You did deliver what you promised. So your reward will be that much greater."

"It will?"

"Yes," White hissed. "I'll kill you quickly."

A single gunshot exploded, and Lexi jerked in reaction, then forced herself to be still while the echoes of it died. She'd be next unless she was very careful.

She heard White speaking, as if to himself. "You sold out your best friend for a price, Mr. Wade. You let me kill his family to cover your own crimes. I knew all along you'd turn on me as well."

Lexi cringed, trying not to envision the bulky Darren Wade lying on the concrete, bleeding, dying as White stood over him, watching with those terrible pink eyes.

And then White's words sank in, and she understood that Connor had been betrayed by his best friend.

The thug was back to dragging her again. Then suddenly there was no floor beneath her anymore. The shock of suddenly falling made her suck in a sharp breath. She couldn't have screamed if she'd wanted to, though because her back slammed onto a hard floor and the impact drove the air from her lungs. Her head snapped backward, hitting concrete. Pain was a blinding white light before her eyes. And that was all.

CHAPTER SEVENTEEN

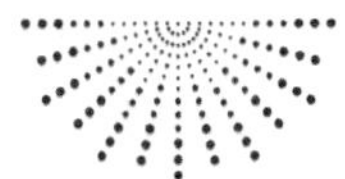

She lifted her head slowly, blinked past the dizziness. Gingerly probing the back of her head, she found a goose egg the size of a golf ball.

She tried to focus on her surroundings, but there wasn't much to see. She was lying on her back on a cold cement floor, in total darkness. Dankness. Forcing herself up into a sitting position, she closed her eyes against the new waves of dizziness washing over the beaches of her mind, carrying things like balance and depth perception away in their brutal undertow.

Okay, just take your time. Get your bearings.

Right. She had to stay calm and stay sharp. She was thinking clearly now.

She'd gotten to know Connor Romano very well in the past few days. Probably better than she'd ever known anyone in her life. He was too sharp not to figure out the truth. He'd have to figure it out. Maybe he'd want to check in on her, or maybe when White never showed up to Connor's planned ambush, it would dawn on him to find out why.

And once he realized his boss had been working for White

all along, he'd know who had her, and he wouldn't give up until he got her back ... or died trying.

That was what she was afraid of. That he'd get himself killed trying to rescue her. Dammit, she couldn't let that happen. She had to do everything she could to save herself before he did something desperate.

Rising, a little unsteadily at first, she moved forward until she felt a cool, rough wall against her palm. Then she ran her hands along the wall and explored the space.

She was in an eight-by-eight square concrete pit. No windows. No doors. No stairs or steps or any possible way out, other than the way she'd come in. She walked every inch of it, in search of anything she could use. Her shins banged against a wooden crate that almost tripped her. Her heart gave a rimshot, *ba-dump-bump*, then settled.

Not now, heart.

She sat down slowly and tried calming herself with mental reassurances, focused on taking deep, slow breaths, and willed her heart not to flip into tachycardia. If she could control her fear, she might be able to control the attack.

And eventually she did.

Then something furry brushed against her leg, and the SVT hit her full force.

There was something in Stryker's eyes when he sidled up close to Romano, something that told him things were going seriously wrong. He sort of meandered as he talked, in a way that appeared aimless, but actually edged them further from the others.

Lexi's half-sisters were watching like hawks.

"The formula's a higher priority than the life of one woman," Stryker said, glancing around to be sure it was safe to talk.

"They think they've pinpointed the location—they're gonna take it out."

"No."

"Drone strike. ETA is about an hour. I owe you, so …" Then he slammed his palm to Romano's chest, shoved a piece of paper and a set of keys into his pocket, and yelled, "That's it, Romano! I want you and these other civilians out of here! Now!"

"Fine, but this isn't over!" Romano shouted back. Then he mouthed "thanks" and, turning, stomped away.

Every cop was looking at him as he went, so he kept up the infuriated routine. When he got close enough to Lexi's family members, he spoke softly. "Get in your cars and follow me. Say nothing."

Kira said, "The hell I'll say nothing. Follow you where?"

"He's taking us to Lexi," Joey whispered. "And I think there's a reason to hurry."

Connor frowned, wondering how the hell she knew that. She couldn't have overheard.

Kira said, "Michael and I will ride with you."

They piled into two cars and took off. As he drove, Connor tugged the paper from his pocket. "This is the address. We have less than an hour to get her out of there."

Kira took the paper from his hand, since she was closest, then took out her phone and started tapping. "Let's see what we can learn from Google Earth."

Connor nodded. He had to get Lexi out of this alive, no matter what it took. Even if it meant letting White walk away.

"I have two weapons," he said. "There might be more in the car. It's Stryker's."

Kira opened the glove compartment. "Make that four guns, and this." She held up a small silver-trimmed crystal flask. Opening it, she sniffed. "Whiskey."

"Yeah, I can modify that just a bit. Shame to pour out the whiskey but—"

"No problem there." Kira unscrewed the cap and took a gulp, then she passed it around.

∼

It took more than thirty minutes for Lexi's heart to convert back to a normal rhythm. She'd tried every trick in the book from carotid massage to bearing down to holding her breath. None of it worked. In the end, she'd done what she constantly warned patients never ever to do; applied pressure to both the carotid and the jugular at the same time, restricting blood flow to and from her brain until she started seeing big fuzzy black spots before her eyes. She was on the verge of passing out when she felt as if her heart was flipping like a pancake.

The painful "BA-DUMP-BUMP" sensation hurt like a heart attack, but wasn't. It was just her ticker converting back to its normal rhythm.

Finally, exhausted, she sat on the floor, her back to the wall, pressing her fingers to her neck to feel her pulse, just to assure herself she was okay.

She was, but she was also weak, dizzy, exhausted, shaky, and her head hurt. Typical aftermath of a major episode.

There was no time to rest, though. She had to get herself out of this mess. Like an answered prayer, lights came on from up above and streamed through the slats in the wooden hatch overhead. It wasn't nearly as distant as it had seemed when she'd been falling through darkness. Which was a good thing, because it was also the only way out.

She got up, grabbed hold of the crate she'd found earlier and placed it in the center of the room. Standing on it, stretching her arms overhead, she could just reach the hatch door. She pushed it upward, testing.

To her surprise, it gave. No locks?

She had to jump and shove at the hatch at the same time to

make it flip all the way open. It banged, her crate cracked, and she cringed at both sounds. But the crate didn't break and no one from above reacted to the noise the hatch had made. More light streamed in now that it was open, making her blink like a mole. Was it morning, or had they rigged up some lighting up there?

She heard voices again, though not as close. She wasn't up high enough to climb out, but she could hop enough to catch glimpses over the edge. She saw two pairs of booted feet moving through a square doorway big enough to drive a truck through. She hopped a few more times, but saw no one else.

The last time she hopped, the crate cracked a little more. Swallowing hard she got off it and stood it up on its narrow end, making it taller than before. It wobbled dangerously as she climbed onto it, first on her knees, then slowly straightening to her full height. This time, her head poked halfway out. The voices were more distant now. Too far away to understand. She could no longer see them. Good.

The crate cracked, all the way through this time. She felt herself going down, and quickly pressed her hands to the edges of the hole to hold herself up. No more crate for help. She pushed herself up and out. It was a struggle, but she did it. Then she lowered the door carefully and ran to the nearest shadowy corner. Hiding there, she listened, watched. The only sound was the rapid, but normal, beating of her own heart and no killers were in sight.

The building was big and empty. Its metal walls reached up high. Over her head, steel grid-like structures supported the roof. Here and there, long fluorescent tube lights gave the place a dull, artificial glow. Some flickered, obviously worn out. The result was eerie and surreal.

Her gaze came down again, locking in on the normal sized doorway in the wall that bisected the building. With a quick glance to her left and right, she tiptoed across the spider web of cracks in the cement floor, gripped the doorknob, pressed her ear to the door. No sounds came from inside. She twisted her hand, and the knob turned.

Her heart in her throat, she stepped into pitch darkness and closed the door behind her.

Her foot hit something soft. Startled, she reached behind her for the door again, pushing it open the merest crack.

Dim light spilled in, and she wished it hadn't. Darren Wade lay on the floor, a neat round hole in the center of his forehead. Dark red streams had painted a bloody headband across his brow. And the whites of his open eyes gleamed in the light. For a second it seemed he was staring right at her.

She was about to lunge right back out of the little room, but she heard White's voice and footsteps. He was coming this way. She spotted another door on the opposite side of the room.

Her decision was made. Silently, she closed the door behind her, then moved forward in the darkness, forced to feel for Darren's body so she could step over it rather than trip and give herself away.

The footsteps came closer. She lifted her hands, palms out, and found the door on the opposite side, located the knob, tried to turn it.

Nothing. It must be locked.

Her heart sank when she heard the approaching steps stop just outside the door she'd entered. White was talking about moving Darren's body. They were coming in here. Desperately she closed both hands around the little round doorknob … and then she felt the protrusion at its center, poking her palm. The lock was on the inside! Deftly she turned it, twisted the knob again. It turned this time, and she slipped through with no idea where she'd emerge, and no time to think about it. The other door was opening as she stepped out. At the last second, she flicked the lock again and closed her escape door behind her.

She'd emerged into another huge section of the building, the front, she thought, separated from the back by a wall and that little office with the body. There were lights on in this side too, but they were flickering and dim. Three men stood in a huddle about a yard inside the big white door, which was closed, and suspended by rollers and a track at its top. None of the men looked her way, but if they did, they would see her. She stood in the open, the door to the small office at her back, and the wide-open space in front of her. Less than fifty feet stood between her and those thugs. Spotting a stack of boxes to her left, she quickly sidestepped and ducked behind them. No one shouted at her. No one seemed to notice.

She crouched there for some time. Behind her, a ladder was mounted to the wall, and she wondered briefly why. Then she forgot all about it, when she heard White's voice. She peered out, saw him coming out of the office and ducked lower behind the boxes. He walked right past her. Everything in her trembled, but he didn't see her. He rejoined the others, the notebook in his hands.

"We need to go. One of the sensors has been tripped. A vehicle is coming this way."

"If it was the FBI, it would be more than one vehicle, boss."

"Yeah," said another henchman. "It could be anyone."

"And it could be Romano," White replied. "Go and get the girl. We might need her." Then he sighed, gazing out through a broken window. "It's going to be a shame to kill him. I've almost enjoyed our ... relationship."

A pattern of beeps came from the huddled group. White pulled out his phone, looked at it. "Too late. He's already here. Get into position. When I give the signal, take him out. Go on."

The men rushed off in different directions. Someone turned off the lights, but there was enough daylight outside now that she could see a little bit.

Two men were scrambling up a ladder just like the one

behind her. They made their way up to a catwalk and then split up, moving until they flanked the big front door.

Lexi looked at the ladder on the wall behind her. That's where it went. Up there, to the catwalk.

Connor was walking into a trap. She'd be damned if she'd sit there and watch as these animals killed the man she loved.

Moving silently to the ladder, she made her way up.

Romano was good, Kira decided. He'd had them leave their car on the main road and pile into the one he was driving, before he turned onto the narrow dirt road that led to the building where Lexi was being held. She'd seen him pour gas into the empty whiskey flask and stuff a rag into the top.

And suddenly the nickname made sense.

It had taken a hell of a lot of arguing to get Cait and Dylan to stay with the rental car at the turnoff. But eventually, they'd agreed. Romano argued that they couldn't risk White escaping because he had a very dangerous weapon with him. He told them to hide the car and wait. If they saw an albino trying to flee, they should try their best to stop him and call Stryker immediately. The good guys should have time to cut White off before he got to the next turn-off.

He left them each a handgun, and Dylan assured him he knew how to use one and would show Cait while they waited.

Kira didn't like it. She'd have preferred Caity and Dylan be holed up in a hotel somewhere. But she figured it was better than having her pregnant sister in the middle of what might become a shoot-out.

Romano stopped the car to let Toni and Nick out. They were to cut through the woods, and emerge on the left side of the warehouse. Joey and her husband Ash rode further and got out, their plan to circle the warehouse and come in from behind.

Then he drove a little farther before stopping again. This time Kira and Mike got out, planning to do the same thing, only they'd emerge on the right. Everyone knew about the planned drone strike. They knew if they heard the buzz of its approach, they needed to get clear of the warehouse fast.

And then he drove on, alone. The most dangerous part of his all-but-suicidal plan was about to unfold.

Kira grabbed Michael by the hand, and they moved fast through the woods.

Lexis heard tires on gravel and the squeak of brakes as a car rolled to a stop outside. She bit her lip and moved faster. At the top of the ladder she pulled herself onto the catwalk. It stretched just above the light fixtures. The gray morning light didn't reach up there, either. She was entirely in shadow.

She could see the shape of the man who'd taken position farther along the narrow platform. It crossed the one she was on like the top of a small t. He crouched like a gargoyle, staring at the doorway as White pulled it open. It was still raining outside. The gargoyle's back was toward her and he cradled a rifle in his arms. If he turned around, he'd see her.

She crouched low and crept inch by inch, not making a sound, not sending a single vibration through the metal to alert him to her presence.

Seconds felt like minutes, inches like miles, but soon the man was within reach. The car she'd heard, and could now see, had stopped about a hundred feet from the front door. Its door opened, and then Connor got out. He had his hands up. He closed the car door with a foot and called out, "I want to make a deal, White. I've got intel."

"I don't think I need your intel, Romano. I've got your woman."

"That's why I'm here. I want her back. And trust me, you need to know what I've got to tell you." Connor took a step closer.

The thug on the right tensed, lifting the rifle to his shoulder and peering through its scope. A few more steps, and Connor would be within his view.

Lexi's body moved as if on auto-pilot. She rose and ran along the narrow I-beam, closing the final few feet so fast her target didn't even have time to turn around all the way before she pushed him so hard, she fell forward. Her chest hit the beam and reflexively, she snapped her arms and legs around it.

The gargoyle wasn't so lucky. He hit the floor and she barely heard the sound of the impact. No one turned to look her way. No one saw the broken body lying below, in the shadows near the right wall. He hadn't even cried out.

She looked at the open doorway again.

"You're not gonna make it out of here alive, White," Connor said. "The Feds know your location. They're coming for you. DEA too. I got here first. I can get you out of this. But only if you let her go."

The gloomy clouds still wept. Misty rain was falling on him. It made a gentle hiss on the roof. Lexi receded into the shadows, back the way she'd come without spending a second on regret. Then she turned at a right angle and crept over the narrow section of metal that spanned the room from side to side. There was another assassin stationed on the opposite catwalk. She didn't have time to be sorry.

～

Romano caught a glimpse of the catwalks on either side as he moved nearer. Dark up there. Probably snipers waiting.

"Tell me what you know, Romano," White said.

Two more men on the ground, besides White. How many up above? he wondered.

Aloud, he said, "Where is she?"

"Within reach," White said, grinning. "I've just sent someone for her. So you'll have a chance to say goodbye."

Romano was bleeding inside, damned distracted by his need to see Lexi, to hear her voice, to know she was still alive. And White knew it, the bastard. He'd drag this out until the drones showed up. Unless he'd already killed her.

No. He couldn't think that way.

"Disarm him," White said.

The two goons came closer, and he stood there with his hands up and let them take his guns. They found them all, leaving him pathetically under-armed—down to just the knife in his boot, and that little whiskey flask, which he'd modified a bit when they'd stopped at the end of the road.

"There's not much time, White," he said, aiming a pointed glance behind him for good measure. "You need to move fast. Let Lexi walk out of here and make your escape. Use me as a shield. It'll work."

Colorless eyebrows rose. White's pale tongue darted out to moisten flesh-toned lips. "I'll keep you both with me. Come in, your woman is waiting."

Romano moved a few steps closer, but he felt a tingle up his spine. Then there was a guttural cry from high above followed immediately by a crash. White jerked his head that way, then nodded at the flunkies who flanked him. "See what's going on. And see what's taking T so long with the girl."

The men moved into the building to investigate.

Great. Only one gun on him now, that he knew of. White's gun. The bastard's gaze was back on him, too. He wasn't even looking for the cause of the commotion. Romano was, though, and what he saw made his blood freeze.

Lexi's unmistakable form was slipping silently down a

ladder from the catwalk. The fellow who'd gone to investigate had his rifle at the ready, but he was looking down, at another man lying on the floor. All he had to do was tip his head up an inch, maybe two, and she'd be dead. One shot. All over. All White had to do was shift his gaze, and he'd see her, as well. In plain sight now, as she moved lower, and he willed her to reach the floor before anyone spotted her.

And then it happened. The goon looked up from the broken body of his dead comrade and he saw Lexi. He lifted his handgun, and a shadow in leather rose up behind him. Kira. One of her hands snapped across his mouth while the other pulled a blade across his throat.

Kira lowered the killer to the floor in silence, took his rifle and slipped deeper into the shadows.

Lexi reached the floor, completely unaware of what had happened, and dashed to the opposite side of the open door, where another man lay, unmoving. She quickly took his rifle and backed into the shadows.

They were sisters, all right.

A soft buzz in started in the distance. Shit, the drones were coming. Seconds were all they had left. And if he so much as moved, White would shoot him. He stood a mere five feet away, gun aimed at his chest. That was point-blank range.

It didn't matter. He had to do it.

"Get out of the building *now!*" he shouted. He dropped low, snatched the knife from his boot and whipped it at the same instant White pulled the trigger.

It felt like a truck hit him square in the chest. He flew backward at the impact, landed hard on the pavement, bleeding. But he had the pleasure of seeing his blade hit home. Blood bubbled from White's neck. Romano's blade had skewered him.

So fast. It had happened so fast. Where was Lexi?

White stayed upright, but was wobbling, his gun hand

shaking wildly as he fought to hold it steady, to aim it at Connor as he lay there helpless ground. He tried to get up and couldn't.

Off to the left, he saw Toni and Nick running out of the building, via some other entrance. To the right, Mike Waters had his kickass bride by the waist, and was racing out of the building, as well.

Lexi was hefting that rifle and walking up behind the albino. "Put the gun down, Mr. White. Don't make me kill you."

His pink eyes met Romano's, and the bastard smiled. Connor read the hate in his eyes and knew exactly what he would do next. White turned drunkenly, and lifted his gun at Lexi. He would take her with him into the grave. He would win, once and for all.

Romano only had one weapon left, the whiskey flask Kira had copped from Stryker's glove compartment. He slid it from his pocket, flicked the lighter and hurled it.

It smashed into the center of White's back and exploded. Flames spread over his back and shoulders. He spun in panic, cut loose a high-pitched, keening wail as he ran, stumbling. His howl was unearthly.

"Connor!" Lexi came running, skidding to him on her knees as a drone came into sight over the tree line.

"Lexi … run!"

She ignored him, tearing his shirt open, trying to see his wound. The drone hovered as White fell burning alive, to the ground. A second drone appeared, and they were about to fire.

And then a pair of nearly simultaneous blasts out of nowhere blew them to bits right there in the sky. Their remains rained harmlessly down to the ground.

Cait, who was supposed to be safely hiding at the crossroads, had a handgun in her hands, still aimed at the spot where the drone had been. Her husband was looking at her like he'd never seen her before. He was also holding a gun.

And then Joey came walking out of the warehouse, holding a rifle, her armed husband at her side.

"Dammit, Connor, be all right," Lexi said, and it wasn't a tearful request but a command.

He tore his gaze from the vehicles now speeding into the area around the warehouse. Federal agents and cops were spilling out of them, pulling their weapons. The sisters dropped their weapons, raised their hands obediently, but their eyes were on him.

"Lexi …"

"Just relax. Don't try to talk." He was bleeding heavily. He could feel the warm stickiness coating his chest and his sides and his belly. Lexi's hands worked feverishly, but he didn't know what she was doing. It didn't matter what she was doing, really. Not anymore. White had shot him in the chest at point-blank range. He was dying.

And it wouldn't be so bad, really. Hell, maybe, if what the faithful of the world believed was true, he'd get to see Justin and little Jack again. God, it would be so good to hold those little angels in his arms, to hear them call him Daddy.

But not yet. Soon, but not yet. He had to tell Lexi …

"Lexi—"

"I said not to talk," she snapped, but there were tears in her voice.

"I want to talk," he told her with surprising force. Then he sucked air through his teeth, because the words had caused him pain. When he spoke again, he kept it quieter, softer. "I love you, Lexi."

Her hands stilled on his chest. She paused to gape at him, then shook her head and began working on him again. "Oh, sure. Now that you're all shot to hell, *now* you love me."

He tried to smile but wasn't sure of the results. Lexi shrugged her coat off and covered him with it. She dragged a metal box over and propped his feet on it. He heard sirens.

"I loved you all along. All that crap … about it not meaning anything…"

"Just trying to get rid of me, huh?"

"I thought … killing White was more … important," he managed to say, and his words were beginning to sound the way they did when he'd had too much to drink. "But I was wrong. I realized it as soon as you left. I was coming to tell you …"

She stared down into his eyes. "You were?"

He tried to nod but felt oddly paralyzed. His entire body had gone numb. "Yeah," he whispered.

He liked it when she ran her hands over his face. And he liked it better when she bent to kiss his lips. Hers were parted and wet and salty with her tears.

Men came running, guns drawn. There were sirens getting louder.

His eyes dropped closed. He was fading fast. He couldn't even feel the pain now. He could still hear, though. He could hear Lexi's smoky voice screaming for paramedics, shouting orders. And he could hear them scrambling to obey. And then there was someone else crouching beside him, and she said, "Who are you? What are you doing?"

"Name's Stryker," he said.

Stryker muttered something else, but Romano couldn't hear anymore. He'd receded to some far-away place where sound couldn't reach. And then suddenly he felt the back of Stryker's hand connect with the side of his face. His eyes flew open and he realized he could feel pain again.

"Stop!" Lexi yelled.

"I'll stop when he's heard what I have to say," he barked. And then Stryker looked him right in the eyes and said, "Your boys are alive, Romano."

Lexi gasped.

"You hear me? Justin and Jackson were not killed in the explosion. They weren't in the house."

"I don't know what you're doing," Lexi said, "but—"

"You were a suspect," Stryker went on, ignoring her. "So was Darren, but I didn't have proof. I knew about Wendy's call to you that day. I knew she and the boys had seen something they shouldn't have. I knew if it leaked your kids were still alive, whoever tried to kill them would try again, and I was half-convinced it was you. So I put them into protective custody."

Connor lifted a hand, and the motion cost him more effort than he'd thought he had left in him. He closed it on the front of Stryker's shirt. "If you're lying ..."

"I'm not."

"You ... kept me from my sons when ...."

"I know. Look, it kept them alive, didn't it?"

Connor's hand went limp and fell to the floor. His eyes closed again. He fought to cling to consciousness ... to life ... and he heard Lexi's voice, tear roughened. "Get out of the way so I can take care of him. We have to get him to a hospital."

After that, he didn't hear anything at all.

CHAPTER EIGHTEEN

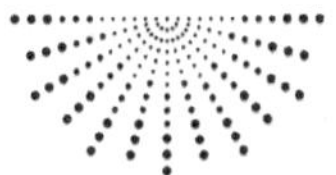

They'd wheeled Connor into the OR, and Lexi asked to go in, but there was no way that was going to happen. Didn't matter that she was a doctor, she was also a mess. She was still arguing when the surgical team closed the doors and wheeled him away, out of her sight.

"Don't die," she whispered. "Don't die, Connor."

A soft hand closed on her shoulder, and she turned, blinking against her tears and seeing a beautiful woman with long wavy hair in every shade of blonde she could think of, looking at her with big, wet eyes. "He's not going to die, Lexi."

"How do you know?"

"Oh trust me," said another female voice. "She knows. It's freaking creepy how much she knows." This belonged to a woman wearing leather, and with short auburn hair that had scarlet streaks.

"She's never wrong," said another, with long dark hair that fell in curls well past her shoulders.

"Not so far, anyway," said a fourth, a petite platinum blonde. She smiled at Lexi's confusion and said, "Hi. I'm Caitlin and I'm your sister."

"We're all your sisters," the first woman said. "I'm Joey."

"Toni," said the one with the dark curls.

"And I'm Kira," said the one in leather. "We all have the same birth father. And uh, we have *a lot* of catching up to do."

Lexi looked at each face, in shades from copper to ivory, and in every one she saw something familiar. "You were there … at the warehouse."

"Yeah. We've been trying to find you," Kira said.

"But you could've been killed."

"But we weren't," she replied with a shrug.

"Come on." Toni slid an arm around her shoulders. "We're gonna take care of you until the surgery's over."

"And you're gonna let us," Cait said.

"At least until the kids get here," Joey added.

"What kids?" Kira asked.

"Damned if I know. I just know there are kids on the way. That Agent Stryker is with them."

Lexi blinked. "Connor's sons. They're alive." She smiled and nodded. "You're right, Joey. He's not gonna die. His boys are alive. Oh my God, it's a miracle."

The first thing Connor was aware of when he opened his eyes wasn't a physical sensation. It was a sense of elation. And for a second he wasn't even sure why he felt it, or what had happened to the shroud of grief that usually greeted him when he opened his eyes.

Slowly, though, he became aware of the dryness of his throat and the pain in his chest. He blinked, bringing the hospital room into focus.

And then it came back to him. Everything that had happened. And that odd fantasy-dream he'd had right at the end. It had seemed so real. God, how much of what he remembered was sheer fantasy, then? Was Lexi really all right? He tried to pull himself up, despite the pain. And he put all his strength into it when he shouted her name.

"Lexi!"

He sat up too fast and had to clutch the mattress to keep from going over the side. And then the door flew open, and he saw her shoving her way past a nurse to get to him.

She stopped near the bed, breathless, her wide brown eyes full of worry. And then she came still closer, sighing in relief. She clasped his shoulders, eased him back down onto his pillows, and then ran her fingers through his hair and said, "Thank God. Thank God, you're all right. You're really all right."

He lay there, trying to wrap his arms around her waist, to cling to her. "I'm sorry," he told her. "I'm sorry, I'm sorry, I'm sorry."

"I know."

"I only wanted you out of harm's way, Lexi. I only wanted you safe. I swear it."

"I know, Connor."

"I love you." He pulled away from her, just enough so he could look up into her eyes. "I love you, Lexi. Give me a chance to prove it to you."

She leaned over him, pressed her lips to his mouth and whispered, "I love you, too, you idiot. And you don't have to prove it to me. You told me all this when you thought you were dying. You got yourself shot trying to rescue me. There's nothing to prove."

He sighed his relief. And then he just held onto her. He needed to. Because the details of that dream were coming back to him now. A dream in which someone had told him the impossible, and he'd believed it because he'd wanted to so very badly. And he'd fought to stay alive because of it.

It hurt to wake up to reality after such a wonderful dream. Even with Lexi's healing love, he didn't think this pain would ever leave him.

She eased away from him. "There's someone waiting to see you."

He closed his eyes. They burned. "I don't want to see anyone but you."

She frowned down at him. One hand came up to cup his cheek, and she plumbed his eyes, his soul. "Don't you remember what Stryker told you?"

His heart skipped. "I … I dreamed that he told me …"

She smiled gently, tears brimming in her eyes. "It wasn't a dream." She stepped backward, reached behind her for the door, pushed it open. And then she turned her head and waved her hand at someone outside.

And a miracle happened.

His two little boys bounded through the door. Justin jumped right up onto the bed and hugged his neck and Jackson stood by the bedside, hopping and reaching for him until Lexi helped him to get on, too. "Careful, your dad's sore. Be gentle."

They were laughing and talking so loudly and excitedly he doubted they even heard her. And the pain of their enthusiastic hugs was the best thing he'd ever felt. For a moment he was stunned, looking down at the little boys who wrapped themselves in his arms.

He lifted his head to look up at Lexi, unashamed of the tears streaming over his face.

He felt them. Their soft, warm skin, and their dark curls. Alive! His little boys were alive! It hadn't been a dream—

"I missed you, Daddy!" Jackson said.

"I missed you too. Both of you."

"I'm glad you're better now, Daddy." Justin searched his face. "We can be together again, now, can't we?"

"We'll never be apart again."

Connor "Molotov" Romano's stony heart melted into a puddle of sheer joy, and tears burned fiery paths down his cheeks. "I love you, boys. I love you so much."

The hugs gentled, but the boys didn't seem willing to move out of his arms. And it was a good thing, because he didn't think he could let go of them if he tried.

Lexi moved to the foot of the bed and cranked it up until he could remain sitting and still lean back against the mattress. She was crying almost as much as he was.

She moved toward the door. "You guys spend some time. I'll check back in later."

"Don't go, Lexi."

She met his gaze, and he saw the love in her eyes.

"You need to be alone—"

"No, we don't," said Jackson. "I want you to stay, Lexi." Then he turned his big dark eyes to Connor, and said, "Lexi's been taking care of us every day since Grandpa Stryker brought us to the hopsickle, Daddy."

"Grandpa Stryker?" he repeated.

Lexi nodded. "The boys have been staying with your friend Monroe Stryker's parents while you've been … recuperating."

"I see."

"It wasn't so bad," Justin said. "They have a pool and a trampoline, and Grandma Stryker makes the *best* homemade ice cream. When Uncle Monroe brought us here, I was so scared at first! I thought you might go to heaven, like Mommy did." He lowered her eyes. "But then Lexi told me you would be okay, and that she would take care of me until you were, and I wasn't scared anymore." He smiled adoringly at Lexi.

Connor figured his expression probably matched that. "You *can't* go, Lexi. Look at us. We *need* you."

Her smile was tremulous. But she nodded and came to join them. She sat on the only available bit of the bed, and Connor wrapped his hand around hers.

"Then I'll stay."

"For always?" he asked her, then he paused, suddenly uncertain. "I know it's a lot to ask ..."

She pressed a finger to his lips, looking at the boys as if she was looking at her very own miracle. Meeting his eyes again, she nodded. "For always, Connor. For absolutely always."

ALSO BY MAGGIE SHAYNE

SMALL-TOWN CONTEMPORARY SERIES

The Texas Brand

The Oklahoma Brands

The McIntyre Men

The Texas Brand: Generations

THRILLERS & ROMANTIC SUSPENSE SERIES

Brown and de Luca Return

The Fatal series

Shattered Sisters

Danger After Dawn

PARANORMAL ROMANCE

The Portal

Wings in the Night

The Immortals

By Magic

ABOUT THE AUTHOR

New York Times and *USA Today* bestselling novelist Maggie Shayne has published 112 novels and novellas for numerous major publishers. She also spent a year writing for American daytime TV dramas *The Guiding Light* and *As the World Turns*. But her heart was in her books, and she'd found it impossible to do both.

Now, she is excited to be publishing with dream-publisher, Oliver Heber Books and she's having more fun than ever.

Maggie lives in a century-and-a-half old farmhouse with two waterfalls outside, in the rural hills of Cortland County NY with her husband Lance, who builds waterfalls for a living, and their dogs. There are always, always dogs.

www.ingramcontent.com/pod-product-compliance
Lightning Source LLC
Chambersburg PA
CBHW050310110726
47899CB00007B/2178